IN THE EYES OF DARKNESS

Joe Freeman

Printed in the United Kingdom.

First Printing, 2020

ISBN: 9781549672255
Imprint: Independently published

this story is dedicated to Jake Powell-Foster.
Who can only be described as the best!

CONTENTS

1

Freddie

The evening had formed a little mist and the cold air was beating over the landscape, the grass turned white on the tips and the leaves of the trees froze and crumbled. Wind from the North blew through his brown hair like Gwenda's soft fingers, his face looked across his land that was already engulfed in the cold winter months.

It was one of the very things in Freddie Peter Martin's life that he loved more than life itself. His plot of land that he inherited from his lovely parents back in '74. Ten years had passed since then, he and his wife had not expected to get the farm. It was a beautiful plot of land, surrounded by thick forestation and by the far left of the house. There was a crystal clear lake, in the summer it was perfect for swimming in to cool off after a long day on the farm. During the winter it would freeze over and expose its frosted colour, the family still liked it all the same. Their home, their land was paradise to them and it was something that they did not want to be taken from them. Freddie was an only child to Marge and Gordon Martin, his darling mother had died during a storm. Her weak heart stopped beating as she sat in her armchair, by morning Gordon found her sat alone. Her skin pale and lips blue. Gordon passed a few months later, some say it was a broken heart that did it. Freddie believed those stories. His father changed and in the month that he died he grabbed Freddie by the hand and said, "Fred. My boy. As my son. My only child and my only boy. This farm is yours when I'm gone. The house, the land, the barn, the small cabin by the barn, the animals. Ha-ha, you can even have the shit that those animals do. But it's yours. Take care of it for me. You can sell the bastard if you want, I won't know I'll be buried in the graveyard next to my darling Marge. As long as this place makes you happy I don't care. Good luck lad."

That was the final conversation they had with each other, about this farm. This land. He could not be happier to have something that his parents had built up. He was almost 55 was Freddie, he was getting on. But, like his father, he refused to even consider the idea of early retirement. He was not yet ready to hand over the farm to his eldest son, Thomas. The boy was a hard worker and a good worker. But the boy would not be able to run this farm without his father's help.

Freddie stood up from the bench he sat upon on the porch and pressed his elbows on the wooden railing. From his jacket pocket, he took out a pipe and pressed it between his lips, there he ignited some tobacco and began to smoke it. It felt good inhaling it and blowing it back out through his mouth and nostrils, he would do it sometimes just to feel the sensation of the smoke blowing out of his nose. The crisp wind blew around the three-story house and he felt it on his face, it pricked his cheeks and he tucked his face into his turtle neck jumper. There wasn't much he could do during the winter months, he could only maintain the animals. The farm would provide corn from the large cornfield on the far right side of the farm near the cobble well. They would sometimes provide meats that they butchered themselves, he used a bolt captive pistol. He pressed it against the skull and pulled the trigger then, POP! A bolt would force itself outwards and impale the animal. Sometimes it would die, sometimes it would not. If not he would be forced to slash its throat.

When everything was ready himself and Thomas would drive into Orington and deliver the goods to each of the shops. This included Mr Shallicker's butchers, Mrs Nixon's dairy and the local supermarket. He was proud of supporting his village and their needs for his goods, in the winter months he could only provide the village with fresh milk. But this was not guaranteed. Due to the harsh weather and bitter coldness, winter was their time off from going into the village. It was hard to drive through the twisting roads and sometimes hard to even drive through the village. Snow would build up on the roads and turn into slush as the cars and other trucks would drive over it, making the roads slippy. Freddie had only one bad experience and he did not want to relive that ever again. He lost control of his truck and crashed into a cobble wall, breaking it. The truck rolled down the hill and slammed into a tree. Freddie was trapped and the cold was only growing more terrible. That was years ago, but he learned a lesson to not drive in the snow. Freddie blew a cloud of smoke from his lips. It was the only warmth he could gather, his wife and children were in the house. Seated around the fireplace, he was planning on getting Thomas and Victor to clear a path to the barn and the cabin. The snow was falling more terrible now, it was only a matter of time before it built up. Its whiteness was surely to lay a blanket over his land, it's smooth crisp white spreading across the English countryside.

The front door opened, it was his youngest daughter Heather. The girl was only four years old, she had her father's hair and mouth but she had her mother's green eyes and soft button nose. She was wearing her jacket, her chin hidden and she wore boots and small purple mittens, "What are you doing out here daddy? It's late. Mummy is doing dinner soon."

He checked his wristwatch, Heather was right it was late. The time was 7:45 pm, she joined him on the porch and stood next to him. Her feet pressed between the wooden bars of the railing that surrounded the porch. She had her head on the top of it and looked out across the land, "It looks nice. Very nice. But it looks better when the sun is shining!"

"It does darling. It does indeed."

"Daddy?"

"Yes, Heather."

"I heard a storm on the telly before. The man said there was going to be a storm."

Freddie looked up at the sky, it was dark and grey there were no clouds but in the distance, he could see that a storm was brewing.

"Maybe there will be. Either tonight or in the morning."

"Oh. I don't like storms."

"I don't either. But remember when your all warm and

toasty in your bed and the snow is falling hard outside. Just remember your warm inside and outside it's all cold and freezing," he had a warming smile on his lips. Heather looked up at him, her face was cute and her cheeks had flushed red from the coldness that battered her face, "Oh yeah! That makes things a lot better now!" "It's what your grandma use to tell me before I went to bed and she knew a storm was coming. Rain or snow it didn't matter. I was scared of them, but once she told me that I was no longer scared of them. There was no reason to be!"

"Yeah! I wish I met Grandma and Granddad!"

"So do I darling. So do I."

"They sound like nice people."

"They were. They would have loved you! Knowing my mum she would have called you her little doll. She always wanted a little girl. You would have been spoiled rotten!"

"Doll? Why would she call me that? It's silly!" Heather laughed as she tapped her hands on the wooden beam.

"Because your small and cute," said Freddie as he ran his hand over the back of her small fragile head.

"Daddy, stop it!" she laughed louder. Her words froze in the air in front of her little mouth.

"Come on. We should be getting back inside. Your mum will want us at the table soon."

"Yeah! I'm hungry. I can feel my tummy crying. I can almost hear it shouting at me for food," she laughed again. Freddie rubbed her head again and ran his thumb over her chin, once he reached her cheek with his thumb he said, "Don't change darling."

They went inside the house, dinner was almost ready.

Victor

He could smell the roast chicken glazed in honey, the vegetables boiling in the pans and the frosting of the chocolate cake his mum had made later in the day. She placed fresh slices of homemade bread in the centre of the table in a small basket, the crust cracked as he picked up a slice. There was a plate in front of each of the chairs of the large dinner table intended to sit eight people.

Victor was the third child to Freddie and Gwenda Martin, he was the second son at the age of 15. He was not like his other siblings in any way, he sometimes felt like he was the odd one out in every activity they took part in, for the simple reason. Victor would rather sit in his room with a horror book in his hands. His room was his own escape from the life that he was born into, he was not like Thomas who was rather handsome and strong. His dad was proud of Thomas, Victor knew that. Victor struggled with many jobs that his dad presented to him, one of which was to climb some ladders in the barn. Victor did not like ladders, it feared him. He felt his knees shake, his hands tremble as he climbed up two steps. His dad would yell at him and call him a fanny for not being able to climb the full steps. As he sat at the dinner table alone, he felt a sudden urge of sadness starting to consume him. It happened every now and again. Even as a child he felt alone, he would play on his own and not join in what Thomas and Edna would be doing. He loved Edna, she was honey to him and she treated him like a human. She would sit with him at mealtimes and ask him about his day, something only his parents would do with him. When he got home from school he would go straight into his room, pull out the book he was currently reading and flick to the last page he read up to. His body would lie on his single bed and he would flick through the pages, his eyes absorbing each of the words he read. His mind consuming the horrors of the story that he read before him. He loved it! Sometimes he would sneak into his parent's room and steal a horror movie and put it into his video cassette. Victor would never feel fear, horror movies never scared him. They were like how his younger sister, Agatha, liked to knit to him. It was something so simple and fun he couldn't help but watch more. His favourite horror movie was Bob Clark's Black Christmas. Under the gore and dark humour, he knew it was just a fictitious story, it was why he liked to read. It was not real, he could place his mind into the mind of the author and see what they wanted him to see. Sometimes a bitter world falling apart, or a dark world that needed light from the heroes of the story. Sometimes they would fail and death would be their end, Victor knew he would close a book or turn his TV off and know it was nothing more than a story. A story that was designed to keep him on the edge of his seat.

Victor remained at the table, he looked across the room and into the living room, his dad would sometimes call it the parlour. And he watched his other siblings talk and laugh with each other. Their voices high and their laughter even higher.

At one point it would have gotten to him, the idea that his siblings could socialise with one another and not involve him. One time that would have hurt him, but not now. He knew he was an introvert, tucked away in the house and placed gently in a drawer out of harm's way. Victor was a handsome young man, he had a boyish

baby face that went with his soft short brown hair.
Yet there was something on his face that he wanted to
hide, but it was part of him now and he knew that it
would never leave him. He was born with a dark brown
birthmark on his face, it covered his small nose and
grew under his eyes. It was one of many reasons why he
was bullied in school. Something he would have to live
with for the rest of his life. If there was one good thing
he could say about himself it would be his eyes. They
were that of sky blue and he was short for his age. He
had a small belly from turning his diet into cake and jam
sandwiches from fresh apples and bowls of wholegrain.
Victor was a frail young thing, from staying up late at
night his eyes had formed dark circles underneath them.
He wouldn't dress like his siblings, he wore shirts and
jumpers and smart pants. They went with his muddy
black Converse. His feet swung quietly under the table,
he kicked the framework and waited for his mum to
notice. Since the dining room was fused with the
kitchen, she was walking around both rooms. She lay
out dishes filled with various foods. The first thing she
laid down was a bowl of garden peas, she put on a spoon
of butter and let it melt on top.
He got a view of the outside, the sky was grey and the
snow was starting to fall softly. By morning the entire
farm would be white, good. It meant he could stay in his
room reading from his book collection. Most of his
books were old, the pages had turned brown and the
spine had cracks on it from the numerous times he bent
the book to read it at a better angle.
"Why are you looking so gloomy Vic?"
Victor looked up, Edna Martin was standing across from
him at the table. She pulled out a chair and sat at it, she

wasn't like the other girls in the family. She was more of a boy rather than a girl, her hair was cut short and her face was well built and although it was manly she was pretty too.

"Oh, I'm just ready for bed. It's been a long week at school that's all," he rubbed his neck.

"Is Peter and his friends still bullying you?"

"What? No! Of course not. Not since mum went to the school and told the headteacher. Nope, no more bullying from Peter or Tim or even Andrew anymore."

"I know you are lying, Vic. Do you want to know how I know your lying?"

"But I'm not lying-"

She cut him off, "You rub your neck."

It was true, Victor had a habit of rubbing his neck when he was either nervous or lying. In this case, he was lying. He continued to rub his neck, feeling his developing hairs growing under his chin.

"Victor. Why do you let them get to you?"

"I try not too, it's easier said than done sometimes you know."

"I can imagine. It's something you can't change. It's just one of those things. A crap hand that life dealt you."

"It's not my birthmark they call me for."

"What is it then?"

"It's the other thing," he looked up at her, his lips forming a nervous smile.

"You mean the thing?"

"Yes. The thing I told you in the barn a few months ago."

The thing that he had told Edna, was something he had not told anyone. He kept it close to his chest and had no intention of letting anyone else know about it. But

15

sometimes words slip.

It started when he started to cry, Edna saw him crying near one of the horses and when she came over he turned away. She had to force the answer out of him and he almost screamed, "I'm gay! You happy now!"

She did not reply, instead, she hugged him and whispered into his ear, "It's okay."

They had kept it a secret, not because of shame or because of embarrassment. It was because Victor was not ready to come out as a homosexual male to his family as of yet. And yet the bullies knew, Peter Jones, Tim Owens, and even Andrew fucking Blaire knew. They all knew, giving them a new reason.

But it was his parents who didn't know.

Gwenda

Gwenda sometimes wished she lived back in her cottage deep in Orington. It was only a wish, a small sweet wish to be surrounded by pink and purple flowers. The smell of Mrs Edgerson's fresh blueberry pie cooling on the windowsill. Or the sound of the trickling fountain her father had made and put it in the back garden. Yet it was only a wish. Not a dream.

Gwenda loved to live in their farmhouse, the land was large and during the summer it was a place of beauty. But in the winter. She hated the winter. She hated the cold and how she could not leave the house in fear of slipping on the ice that glazed over the porch. The land became nothing but a place of blandness with only three colours, white, grey and black. It made her feel depressed, coping with these colours for over four months as it infected her land and made her mood shift. It also made her prone to snapping at her dear children who she loved dearly. All five of them were perfect in her eyes, all perfect and beautiful children. She wasn't one for picking favourites but if she could it would be her first son. Thomas. He was just 18 and was already becoming a man he had a pretty girlfriend. Thomas was going to take the farm when they passed to the other side and he was going to make the best out of it as he could. He dropped out of school when he was 13 to help out more on the farm, he had worked every day since then. Gwenda watched him as he grew into more of a man as each day passed.

Gwenda was born 47 years ago to Mary and John Swan, she had grown up in Orington and knew the older residents quite well. She had grown up being called Gwen by her friends and her parents were the only ones to call her Gwenda. Her parents were still alive, they had stayed in that little cream coloured cottage and had intended on keeping it that way. She met Freddie when she turned 19, she was at the local pub, The Crossbow, and saw a rather handsome man sitting at the bar. She walked over to him and the pair spoke freely, she told him she wished to see him again. Freddie told her she would and he wrote his house phone number down on a napkin. Gwenda still had the napkin, tucked away in a biscuit tin along with other important items of her life. Including her first engagement ring that turned out to be too big but she kept it anyway. It was filled with photographs of her children, she had a small box inside too. And inside that was her children's first teeth that they lost.

When she thought about it she knew she was a silly woman for even considering keeping such things. But one day her children would leave this house, it would be a big empty house. She dreamt of all of them getting married and having beautiful children of their own. She would be happy to be a grandmother and raise her grandchildren the same way she raised her children. Gwenda liked to plan ahead, it was one thing she liked to do but knew she shouldn't. As life was filled with unexpected twists and turns. One day she might not even wake up at all. Freddie had taught her that, Freddie had taught her many things in her life. But most importantly he taught her to not take life too seriously.

That was the case with most things she had done with her life. She was tasked with the meat side of things, she would never butcher the animals that was left to Freddie and Thomas. She would dispute the meats evenly into the packaging and place it inside of cardboard boxes and place them in the freezer.

Her figure was that of a middle-aged woman, although her body aged and her hair had started to become grey at the roots. It was her hazel eyes that sparkled, her husband loved her eyes. He would look into them before they kissed and before they made love. She wore a house dress and a light blue apron, when she was not working in the kitchen she would be in the cornfield. Snapping the corn from the stalks and stripping them down exposing them to their cobs. She had her mother's hair, it was long and auburn she mostly tied it in a bun and kept it out of the way of her sweating face.

Gwenda knelt down by the oven and pulled out the bronzed chicken, she put it on the counter and rested her oven gloves next to it. She dipped a brush into the pot of honey and glazed the skin, making sure to get in between the legs and the wings of the bird. Her husband entered the kitchen, she could tell with how he walked and how he breathed as he entered. He grabbed her waist and kissed her neck softly.

"It looks delicious Gwen," he exclaimed as he ran his finger through the honey. She slapped his hand away.

"No. Not yet. Go and place the potatoes and sweet corn on the table will you. It will save a lot of time. Also, can you shout Thomas when you have a minute? He's upstairs with Michelle."

"Is he now? He's probably almost balls deep in her now Gwen," Freddie laughed. All Gwenda could do was give a shocked laugh at her husband and she said, "Freddie! How could you say such things?"

"I just open my mouth and it comes out!" he laughed at his sarcasm.

"You need to keep your bloody mouth shut about him and Michelle. You know how much he thinks of her."

"I know. He sorts her out alright. I've seen how she is around him. I don't know what that lad does but he must know how to use it. Either that or his tongue is fast."

"Freddie Peter Martin! Now that's enough. That is your lad you are talking about."

"Yes, it is. And who do you think he comes to asking for advice? You? Or me?"

"He's asked you?"

"Of course he has. He's a lad. I'm his dad at the end of the day. If he didn't come to me I would be upset. You wouldn't tell him the right things. I won't beat him around the bush. I'll him exactly what he needs to know."

"Well I am shocked there," said Gwenda as she handed Freddie a dish of mashed potatoes.

"Go on. Put it on the table and tell your children to sit down. I still want you to shout Thomas. Tell him his dinner is ready," he smiled and took the dish over to the table, once he put it down he said,

"Come on. Dinner is ready. Sit down," he walked out of the dining room and headed towards the stairs. She heard him shout, "Thomas! Dinner!"

Gwenda picked up the chicken and headed over to the table. She placed it in the centre, her children were arguing over what they wanted to eat.

"Can you not argue at the table, please? No! Agatha! Don't hit your sister. Oh, come on Heather use a fork, not your hands! Dear me!"

"It was her. She started it first," shouted Agatha, her long hair swinging in the air.

"I do not care who started it. Please don't slap her."

Heather grabbed her mashed potatoes with her small hands and began to stuff them into her mouth. Some of it fell onto the table and some landed on the floor and made a small splattering sound.

"Freddie, will you give Heather a spoon please?"

Freddie didn't answer verbally, instead, he just nodded and took a small spoon from the centre of the table and handed it to Heather. He said, "Come on Heather. You're four now. No need to start using forks and spoons to eat,"

Every time the family would sit down for a meal there would be arguing and messing around, sometimes it was peaceful. And Gwenda would not change a thing.

Because at the end of the day, they were all family.

Thomas

When they spent their first time together they had almost drunk themselves to death. Thomas Peter Martin had only touched alcohol the once and that was when he stole a bottle of bourbon from his dad's cupboard. It was always locked but he had located the key and managed to steal a bottle, he knew his dad would not miss it. This was over two years ago and he had not touched the stuff since.

He had grown up in a farm environment, lifting heavy boxes and guided the animals into the barn when need be. The pigs oinked at him as he fed them the leftover vegetable scraps from the kitchen and he learnt how to ride a horse thanks to his dad.

Due to his heavy lifting and his mum's healthy meals she provided for all of the family he had a well-toned body, his four-pack was turning into a sick-pack and his biceps were getting bigger.

The trouble to some, not to him, was he had fallen in love at a young age. It had been the butcher's daughter in Orington, sweet Michelle Shallicker. He noticed her when he was taking boxes of beef and pork into the butchers. She was sat at her father's desk, her hair long and curly blonde. She wore a pair of silver-rimmed glasses but the first thing he noticed was none of those. It was her emerald green eyes, his eyes shifted down her body. Looking at her small but perky breasts and down to her large milk coloured legs. She noticed him but at first, he wasn't sure if she had the same intentions as himself.

Over the next three weeks, he had gotten to know her, learnt that she was quite shy but once he had gotten to know her she became a real pleasure to speak to. They had gotten to know each other very well, as soon as his dad parked the truck up at the back of the butchers Michelle would already be there waiting for them. Waiting for him. At that point he was just a sixteen-year-old boy, three years out of secondary school, he had not yet learnt the girl's age. She looked young, maybe his age or a year younger. But as his time with her grew, he learnt from her dad what her real age was. And it surprised him "Our Michelle is eighteen and the girl can still slice open a pig as if it was a fucking cake!" he was shouting at one of the younger members of the butchers. He struggled with stabbing a pig.

The age knocked him back a little, but he learnt to not care. Why should he after all? The two got on like a house on fire. She must have liked him, he asked her if she was busy one afternoon and she said no. So Thomas invited her for some coffee and a walk in the park. He wanted to tell her he liked her and ask her out on a date, he knew as the man it was his duty to do so. They got some coffee and took a stroll through the park. The midday sun was hot and hammering down on the small village. He felt a little uncomfortable just saying that he liked her, but when they shared a laugh her hand touched his thigh and stayed. It wasn't long, it couldn't have been for more than three seconds but to him. It felt like thirty minutes. So Thomas asked Michelle out on a date, as he had expected or more so hoped. The girl said yes.

Within a month the two had managed to stay together, they had met each other's parents but one night would stay with him forever. No matter what happened to the two of them. This one night, when there were no clouds in the inky sky, they were at Thomas' house. They were sat on the porch when she said to him, "Thomas. Do you have any alcohol?"

"Yes," he didn't waste any more time. He rose and headed into his house. The time had just gone 8:00 pm, he found the key to the cupboard and unlocked it. There he removed a full bottle of bourbon. He relocked the cupboard and put the key back where he found it. Placing it on the nail above the cellar door. When he went outside she giggled, so he said, "Come on. Let's go to the barn, it will be lit by the moon."

The moon was high in the field of darkness, it was shining a bright white and could not be missed. Even if you tried to avoid it.

The two of them scurried over to the barn hand in hand, Thomas pulled open the door and the two of them slipped inside. Once they were inside he closed the door and told her to climb the ladder, he came up after her and looked up her dress. Seeing her black underwear and part of her buttocks, he suddenly felt a throbbing in his pants. They lay side by side on the upper part of the barn, it was almost impossible to stand up without hitting your head on the roof. They had taken the ladder to the second platform, the first platform could be walked across, this part was more for storage.

He peeled away the plastic and popped the lid off before taking his first mouthful, it was strong and burnt his throat. But he liked it.

They shared the entire bottle and both got drunk.

They kissed drunkenly and he was sure he did it wrong, then they held each other. If he was doing it right, he thought he was, he was sure they do a lot more than just hug one another. Michelle then did something that he wasn't expecting to happen as early, she started to unbutton his shirt with one hand. Whilst her other slipped down his jeans, he felt her hands stroke over his erect cock. Her thumb rubbing the head softly, it was his turn to do his part. He kissed her with the same motion as she did. One of his hands cupped her small breasts, he massaged it and he would pinch the nipple. He discovered she was not wearing a bra under her dress. His other hands worked it's way up her thigh and over her vagina, he began to rub it as softly as he could. Treating it like a frail piece of china.

Once they were both naked, she pushed him down gently and climbed on top of him, her legs resting on either side of his waist, she grabbed him and slipped him inside of her. He made a gasping sound as he held her, once her thighs met his waist he felt more relaxed then she slurred her words, "I'm...I..hurting you?"

He shook his head and said, "No, of course, your not," he stroked her cheek and let his hand slip down her body.

"Are you sure? I'll stop if you feel uncomfortable."

He shook his head once more and she smiled back at him. It was his first time.

Weeks passed and turned into months, the month's interwind into years and nothing had changed between the two.

Yet the vile rumours started to spread, the vile and vulgar rumours that Michelle Shallicker was a whore. It started quite sudden with some people from Victor's year shouting at them as they held hands. One of them shouted, "Look who he's fucking. Michelle Cock licker!"

Thomas passed on that they were just kids with nothing better to do with their time, but when the adults started saying things. A great deal of concern began to wander within his mind. He pushed it away as just plain jealousy that he had a pretty blonde for a girlfriend but it continued.

It got worse when his mum sat him down and asked him if the rumours were true. He told her they weren't but he had heard it so many times he was no longer sure if he was just kidding himself.

Then he confronted Michelle, she told him it was because she was dating a boy two years younger than herself. One day things got worse when a boy who used to go to school with Thomas threw a stone at her head calling her a whore. He grabbed his crotch and thrust into the air shouting for her to suck him off. Thomas had had enough! He charged at the boy and tackled him down, he wrapped his hands around the boy's throat and pounded the back of his head in the road. Screaming and shouting, "Stop it! Stop it!," he looked up at people passing by and shouted even louder until his throat hurt, "All of you fucking stop it! Stop it now!"

He had hurt the boy badly, causing the back of his head to bleed but he didn't care. The rumours began to go dim, but the odd word would circulate now and again. Thomas still didn't care. He loved Michelle Shallicker and that was it!

"Thomas! Dinner!"

He shook his head and looked down his bed, Michelle was sat on the edge fixing her hair by looking in the mirror, "Oh. I'm starving!" she said as she rubbed her stomach.

"Same love. Come on."

Edna

Tomboy.

That was Edna Martin, she was a Tomboy and she was more than happy to be called it. Her hair was cut quite short, cut shorter than a girl would normally want to have it. All she did was look at her self in the bathroom mirror and snip the long parts of her hair away. She would ask her mum to cut the back and tidy her hair up a bit if need be. Her mum wasn't fond of her daughter's views on her own appearance, but she would not intervene in any of her children's lives.

It came to Edna that she would prefer to have short hair when she was playing football with Thomas. The long brown strands covering her eyes, she decided to enter the bathroom and take out a large pair of scissors. She snipped at the sides of her hair first, pulling it down and slipping the strands between the two blades. She grunted each time she snipped some away, the long brown hair was clogging the drain in the sink. The hot water would wash some of it away each time she let some fall.

Her mum walked in on her and gasped at her daughter's new look. Edna had no words and neither did Gwenda. Instead, the two of them just looked at each other with soft expressions.

Gwenda said, "Come here."

Edna did as she was commanded, Gwenda took her daughter's hand and removed the scissors.

"You look a mess," Gwenda opened the scissors and started to tidy up the mop of messy hair. It had been cut unevenly. Especially around the back of her head, "You can be silly sometimes Edna."

Gwenda said as she snipped.

"It was getting in my eyes mum. It's been annoying me for years," said Edna as she looked down so her mum could get a better view.

"You have beautiful hair, Edna. Beautiful and long."

"I do like my hair. I just don't like it long."

"Do you like a boy?" asked Gwenda suddenly.

"What? No, of course not. I just want it to be cut short."
"Are you sure? I use to change my appearance to attract boys. I never helped. Made them turn away from me," Gwenda laughed.
"I don't like any of the boys in Orington mother. I just want my hair to be cut short," Edna was getting annoyed now, she could sense it in her own tone.
"I was only asking. Now stay still, I have nearly finished."
The scissors snipping became less and less, once Gwenda was finished she said, "There. It looks much better. Have a look."
Edna looked at herself in the mirror and she felt a smile flash across her thin lips, she liked it! No, she didn't like it, she loved it! Her mum had done a good job it was neater and fitted around her head like a motorbike helmet.
"Thank you, mother."
"You are a welcome sweetheart."
She looked at herself once more, admiring her new hairstyle.
That was two years ago, the only thing that had stayed the same was her hairstyle. She no longer trusted her mother, things had changed. The two of them had grown apart over the last two years. Edna could not say exactly what had caused her relationship with her mum to start to fall apart. There were numerous factors that could contribute to it.
But the main thing that had gotten to her was her relationship with one of the Rogers'. To Gwenda the Rogers family was pure filth, they were the lowest of the low. The eldest of the two children was Marie Rogers. She was probably the best member of the family. That

was saying something!

The parents were crude and horrific people, Gwenda did not even allow any of her children to spill their names in her house. The parents owned Rogers mechanics on the far side of the village, everyone knew their names. It was Rita and Zack Rogers. Then there was Francis Rogers the only son. He was like his father, tall, bulky, crude and greasy. And Edna had fallen for him!

She had met him whilst she was in Orington, she was minding her own business when she met him. Francis was seated on a bench in the park, his large arms crossed and in-between his lips was a cigarette. He would occasionally uncross his arms to allow his lungs some fresh air. But only for a split second. His black hair looked to be covered in a thin layer of natural hair grease. Edna found out later it was in fact hair gel, the boy had used a lot of it. She found out his age whilst talking to him, he was no boy at all. Francis Rogers was a man, he was 26 years old when she met him. And Edna was just a 15-year-old schoolgirl. They spoke and laughed with one another, she went red when she saw him unbutton his boiler suit. It was the summer, after all, he must have been hot. She also noticed how large his hands were and how dark the hair was. She found it attractive, a hairy man.

"Oh, I am sorry. It's getting hot,"

She ran her hands over her thighs and to her knees and said, "Don't worry. You are right, it is hot!"

She was sweating for two reasons, the sun's blistering heat was starting to get unbearable. The second reason was Francis Rogers. She couldn't quite think why she found the man attractive, he wasn't exactly handsome. If anything he seemed to have average looks. Then he said,

"Do you want a milkshake?"

Their relationship had started.

For three months they were with each other every weekend, she had forced herself to lie to her parents and told them she made friends. She was a loner after all. So her parents didn't question anything, they believed their daughter was sleeping over at one of the girls' houses from school. Edna had turned sixteen in them three months, they had kissed one another and he was gentle with her. He never once forced himself onto her, not once! The rumours of Francis hurting girls and forcing his large hands on their bodies was nothing but bitter lies!

Edna hated her parents for that, she could never forgive them. She had wanted to sleep with him for some time now, but could never think of a way of asking him. She didn't want to seem forceful but at the same time, she didn't want him thinking she didn't love him. One night she decided to go through with her plan.

Edna started to crawl on her hands and knees towards him as he sat on the edge of his double bed. She grabbed his knees and started to kiss his legs, she began to unbuckle his belt and all he did was look at her with a shocked expression on his face. She could only smile but she felt her eyes tearing up, she stopped when she unbuckled his belt and removed it. She began to cry and her head pressed into his thigh, he rubbed her hair and said, "Edna, it's okay."

"It's not okay. I just want to make you happy," she said with tear-filled eyes.

"You are! Just by being with me you make me happy, come here."

She lifted her head and sat next to him, her head tucked

deep into his bulky chest. He hushed her and she
continued to cry. When she was ready to continue her
hands trembled and shook as she started to take off his
vest. He didn't let her, instead, he grabbed her wrists and
pushed her hands away softly. He removed his vest
himself. His chest and stomach were hairy but only
lightly, she could still make out his abs. She felt her eyes
starting to dry up as a wave of happiness started to
consume her body. "Edna, if you don't want to. Don't.
You don't need to do this to make me happy you know."
"I know Francis. But I want to do it. With you,"
She brushed her hand on his cheek and kissed him. As
she started to pull his pants down his hands removed her
shirt and skirt. He placed them on the floor and looked
at her, his eyes were that of the sky and the pupils began
to expand. She wore a white cotton bra and although she
was only sixteen she was rather busty for her age. He
was amazed.
She rubbed his penis, her hand trembling as she felt it
grow in her hands. The only thing stopping her from
feeling the skin was his underwear. His finger was
stroking her inner thigh, he slipped his finger inside of
her and she moaned, not from pain. But from pleasure.
When she knew he was grown she said, "Do you want to
put it in?"
He held her face with his hands, he cupped her small
head and he said, "Yeah...okay."
She climbed on top of him and unclipped her bra, letting
it fall on the floor. She removed her underwear and he
removed his. She saw it. Her face changed she couldn't
help but notice how big he was. It scared her. But she
wanted him.
She grabbed it, and inserted it inside of her. She felt it go

in and although it hurt she felt pure pleasure at the same time. She moaned loudly and Francis said, "Shit! I'm sorry. I'll be gentle. I'm so sorry Edna,"

She cupped his face this time and kissed him, she bite his bottom lip making sure not to bite too hard and said, "It's okay. It's fine."

She let herself slip his full length inside of her, it hurt like hell but she was more for the pleasure and love for Francis over anything else. She began to ride him, her small hands on his face and shoulder. His large hands were on her waist, sometimes they would tickle her back.

When he came she felt his fluid inside of her, she felt him slow and he pulled himself out of her.

He then asked, "I didn't hurt you did I?"

"A little. But the pleasure was more thrilling for me. It was...it was really nice Francis."

She rubbed his face and kissed his lips once more.

That was the last good memory she had of Francis Rogers, after that he changed. Three months down the line she found out she was pregnant she had missed herself bleeding for those three months. She knew she was carrying a child, she spoke to Francis about whilst they were at the park. They were standing at the top of a hill. Cobble stairs on each side and in the middle there was a water fountain.

"What?" he said, his tone had shifted from the gentle giant to that of a monster. He almost growled at her.

"I said I am pregnant. I think I'm three months. It could be less," she said.

"How? Why? How could you do this to me?"

"Do what? Get pregnant. We both know how it works Francis. You put your penis into me and you cum into

31

my vagina-"
"Edna! If anyone finds out I am the dad of that baby I
will lose everything. There is almost a ten year age gap
between us. You need to get rid of it!"
"That is not your decision to make!" she turned and
walked towards the stairs.
"Edna wait!" he ran up to her and grabbed her by the
wrist.
"What?" she spat at him.
"I'm sorry. But please listen to me. I want to start a
family. Just not yet. I'm not ready and neither are you!
Please just let us talk about it at least."
"Francis I-"
"Let me finish please," he didn't wait for her
confirmation he continued, "I want to have a baby with
the one I love. I have only ever loved one person."
She looked at him "I'm sorry Francis. I know you love
me and I love you too. I just can't!"
She turned on her heels and started to walk down the
stairs, that was when he did it. Did something that would
change Edna's life forever.
He gave her a mighty shove, his strength was too much
for her frail and tender body. Edna fell backwards, she
lost her footing and fell down the stairs. Each step broke
something or caused something to bleed.
When her body came to a rest she was lying across the
last three steps, her forehead was bleeding. Her right
arm was broken and she had cracked six ribs. Some of
her teeth had been knocked out of her.
She was rushed to the infirmary, they had concluded she
was pregnant. She had lost the child during the fall. Her
mother had found out what she had done and the
bitterness had started within her family and the Rogers'

family.

Agatha

She left the house through the back door. She closed it quietly behind her, her cold breath came out in front of her. She rubbed her gloved hands together it created a surge of warmth. Her feet pressed hard into the snow and it crunched beneath her boots. She had been talking with her sisters at the dinner table, the school was always the topic of interest at the dinner table. Victor and Edna never spoke about school, the two of them seemed to be the types of people to be bullied. Victor did have the large birthmark on his face, children could be personal and be cruel with their words. She knew that much but other than that she could not think why Victor was bullied he was such and sweet person to be around. As for Edna, he was a weird teenager. She spent most of her time in her room humming and looking through old photographs or finding new styles that suited her. Although Agatha was the daughter of Freddie and Gwenda Martin she wasn't a pretty girl like Edna or Heather. Instead, she was a rather ugly little girl, her hair was messy and had no colour as if it had been bleached. Her eyes were grey and her skin was pale and had acne spread across her cheeks. Her lips were always peeling and she had pink stains where she constantly licked her lips. Agatha Martin was also short for her age, she had a plump body and her arms were small and her hands were fat.

She walked across the field and headed towards the gun range. The whole walk there she kept her hands tucked into her pockets. Her face was half-hidden in her jacket so she could smell her lavender perfume. The walk was brisk, the night air was cold and the sky was a dark blue but turning black. The walk to the gun range was a long one, it took more than 15 minutes and in weather like this, it could take 20, sometimes even 25 minutes. The gun range was built close to the tree line, the forest spread all across Orington. They were somewhere close to the start of it. The trees had lost most of their leaves. Making the trees look like arms clawing out of the soil, the branches like bony fingers trying to grab at something.

Once Agatha reached the gun range she sighed deeply, it was getting cold and she just wanted to be tucked into her bed now. A warm cup of tea by her side as she watched the snow start to fall outside, it was mid-November. It meant only one thing.

Christmas wasn't far away now. It was her favourites time of year.

Agatha looked over the countertop of the gun range. There was no guns or knives left behind. She was glad. Carrying those heavy things back to the house would have been a task, especially in this cold air that was consuming her. As she lifted her body she heard something coming from the trees. She slowed down as she lifted herself upwards, the forest was plunged into darkness. The wind whispering around her and it gave her a sense of unease. She wanted to know what the noise was, an animal? Perhaps, but the noise would normally continue or she would be able to hear it faintly in the distance. Agatha took once step back, the snow crunched behind her. And it crunched in front of her followed by something tapping on a tree. Like fingers, she had to squint to fully see what she was looking at. That was when she saw it.

Two hands wrapped around the tree as if someone was climbing the incline at the tree line. Her eyes went wide. The hands let go and began to climb up the hill, she could not see a face or a body. Or even arms. Just two hands beginning to crawl upwards towards her. Agatha was frozen in fear.

She only reacted when she felt something grab her from behind, forcing her onto the floor. She let out a cry and screamed, "Get away from me!"

A feeling of cold began to consume her skull, she kept her eyes closed tightly.

But when she opened them, there was nothing there.

Hugo

He was one of two farm handlers that Freddie and Gwenda Martin had hired for their farm. They weren't normally needed during the winter months due to very little work. But their parents had gone to the North-West. They were spending their winter with the Martin family. Hugo Brent was the youngest of the two brothers who were hired, he was just 25 years old. They had been working on the farm for five years now and had enjoyed working here.

He lived in the small cabin with his older brother, Richard, although they were brothers. The two of them hated each other, Hugo had grown a strong hatred towards Richard. But he had grown a strong bond towards a member of the Martin family. It was Gwenda Martin. The two of them had gotten on very well since they first met, the two of them enjoyed reading. Especially, now Hugo was almost ashamed to admit it, a good romance novel. He didn't know what he loved about them. Maybe it was the very idea of falling in love, it was something he was sure he had done but never experienced with another person that he would like to admit. He was only young, his father would have told him to get a grip and that falling in love at 20 was just lust. Saying he just wanted the girl to spread her legs for him. That was not the case for Hugo. He had many things going for him, he wasn't ugly but he wasn't handsome either. His bottom lip was quite fat and always wet. His nose was small but it was hooked, he had long eyelashes that fluttered when he blinked. It gave him the nickname camel in secondary school. A nickname that he wasn't very fond of. His hair was a mop of strawberry blond that hung down over his eyes sometimes. Getting caught in those long eyelashes. His build was small and he was rather skinny for a young man of his age. When he was a teen Hugo suffered from severe acne, it spread far across his face and chest. His face had turned into a breeding ground for pimples and blackheads that clogged the pores on his cheeks and nose. Eventually, the acne faded but it left his face scarred forever, small dints littered his cheeks. Giving him a new appearance, but that was over three years ago now.

Once he moved onto the farm the bullying stopped and he got on very well with the eldest son, Thomas. They were both a similar age when Hugo was hired by Freddie. So it was only natural for the two to form a bond, the bond didn't last long. Thomas started to dedicate most of his time to his girlfriend, Michelle. She was a pretty one and was only a few years younger than himself, sometimes when he scrubbed the floor of the barn or fed the horses he saw her sitting on the porch. She was normally reading a small hardback book as she

gazed at those pages through those glasses of hers.
Hugo wasn't interested in Michelle.
Since himself and Thomas had grown apart over the
years Hugo had formed the bond with Gwenda.
One day whilst he was in the house collecting his money
from Freddie, he couldn't help but notice the rows of
hardbacks on the shelf in the living room And Gwenda
was seated in her leather armchair reading one of them,
that was how it all started.
She offered him a book to read and unexpectedly, to her
at least, he took a romance novel. Hugo hid it under his
arm and thanked, he read the over 300-page story in two
days. Once he returned it, Gwenda offered him some tea
from the pot. Freddie was out and his children were
either in their rooms or in the barn.
"I really should be going Mrs Martin. I think Rick needs
me help with barn. There's shite all over the place, needs
scrubbing up it does."
"Oh never mind all that," she said as she poured him
some tea as she filled two of the cups she said,
"Sugar? Honey? What about lemon?"
"One sugar..." he said with defeat.
He sat himself down across from her on the couch, he
gripped his flat cap tightly in his hands as his thumb
began to massage the fabric. Gwenda handed him the
cup on a saucer and he thanked her again, then she said,
"So, you like love stories do you then Hugo?"
"I do like um me. I just like how people fall in love and
all that kind of stuff. It's kids stuff if I'm honest. But
can't help liking it can I?" his accent was strong.
"No, I understand what you are saying. It's all part of a
good read I think. Tell me, Hugo. What did you think of
the book then?"

"Oh, it was a bloody good' un weren't it? Ending was a bit shite but I guess that is how the writer wanted it to end," he sipped his tea and his eyes were drawn to the plate of yellow cakes on the table.

"You have an accent. Where are you from Hugo?"

"Well me and me family aren't from Orington. Oh no. We are from the North-West of England. Came up here when I was just a baby." He pronounced baby as babie.

"What made you move up here then?"

"Work. Me dad worked down pits but he couldn't be doing with it no longer. It was getting on top of him. As he was surrounded by all coal powder and all that kind of shite he got a bad cough. Oh aye, he did Mrs Martin. Should have heard him some nights. Sounded like he was tryin cough up a new car the way he carried on," he laughed a little. He was happy that his dad was feeling better now.

"That's good. Would you like to take another book with you? You can pick any you like," Gwenda sipped her tea and licked her lips as she pulled the cup away.

"I would love too."

He stood up and picked a new book, he sat with her until the pot of tea was empty and the conversation had run dry, he thanked her before leaving. But that night as he lay in his bed, the hardback book in front of him he could smell her sweet perfume. The smell made him feel bubbly inside, and his jeans went tight where his crotch was.

Richard

"You stupid shit!" said Richard Brent as he began to button his shirt as he looked at himself in the mirror. He admired his looks. The man was the eldest out of himself and Hugo, the eldest by 8 years. Although he knew he was ugly, his face was that of a frog and he had the neck of a turtle he took great pride in his appearance. His hair was combed neatly to the side, and his crooked teeth were always clean. Not to mention he always smelled nice as he washed himself every day. Working on a farm made you smell awful. Sometimes he would gag at the smell of himself and would need to bathe almost right away. Luckily the Martin's had provided him and his brother with a working bathtub. The small cabin was once a large shed, but Freddie and himself converted it into a place of accommodation. He was more than proud of what he had done. Richard ran a comb through his hair, trying to untangle any knots.

"Are you going out tonight?" asked Hugo as he flicked through the pages of a book he held. Hugo was lying across his single bed, his gaze focused on the words.

"I am. Going to the Crossbow," he said as he used his fingers to push down his hair.

"What for?"

Richard stopped what he was doing and turned around to his brother, "I'm going to get my hair cut. Why do you think I'm going pub Hugo?"

"Knowing you you'll get a fucking haircut at the crossbow," Hugo kept his thumb on the last word he read.

"I'm going to pull some skirt, aren't I? You stupid mong," Richard said as he smelled his wrists. His aftershave was strong and smelled sweet.

"You couldn't pull a door, Rick. What makes you think you can pull some skirt?"

"Why not? Why don't you come with me? I'll show you how it all works shall I?" he lifted his eyebrows.

"You? Show me, how to pull some skirt? Don't make me laugh Richard Brent," Hugo sniggered.

Richard only grunted before leaving the cabin, he slammed the door closed behind him.

As soon as he was outside he took out a packet of cigarettes from his breast pocket and lit it. The tobacco inside of the paper began to burn. It turned bright orange as he inhaled. A light grey smoke trailed from his lips, before disappearing into the night air. He looked over at the main farmhouse, it was a big thing. Three floors and an open attic, it was big enough for the family that lived behind the walls.

He walked up the path that was covered by the snow, it crunched under his feet. He got to his car, his fingers fumbling for the keys in his jeans pockets. Once he pulled them out he heard something coming from the barn, it didn't sound like one of the animals. Richard turned his body to face the barn, there was nothing but the deathly silence as the cold air burnt his cheeks and knuckles. He shook it off as the wind creaking through the barn. It was old, the wind was going to get through the wooden planks that made the barn up.

He climbed into his car and stuck his key into the ignition and twisted it. The car's engine rumbled and the headlights created a beam of light across the farm. Exposing the cornfield. He turned the steering wheel and started to drive towards the gravel road. Then the car stalled.

It jolted forward and it lost power, he stuck the key back into the ignition and twisted. The engine did no start. He cried, "Fuck me!" and slammed his hands on the wheel. The isolation had already begun.

2

1

It was just after midnight when it began. The dreams
that began to unwind within those who slept on the
Martin farm. The dreams flooded their minds with
darkness, the heavy knocking on their skulls. The cold
air blowing over their skin making it get tighter. A loud
knocking like the sound of beating drums invaded their
ears, yet not one of them woke up from their deep
slumber. A fitting rage of terror was building around
them. Even the dogs that slept near the burning ember.
A knocking only continued, even in their slumber they
felt awake. And watched by blind eyes, something
sinister about blindness stalking. It lurked within them
as it started to interwind itself among them. Choosing
them, one by one. Wondering what it should do. How it
should do it. It was one of a thousand minds, a thousand
thoughts and a thousand eyes. Each watching the Martin
farm. The body oozed that of insanity and a deep
craving of requiem of which it wished so dearly for. Its

body was that of synthetic flesh that seemed to breathe like a set of lungs. Once it managed to get into the thoughts it was when it began. When it truly began...

2

Although the morning had emerged the sky was still dull and it exposed the thick snow that had built up last night. The farm was now that of whiteness, the sun was not shining like it did yesterday. Saturday morning had brought a gloomy day for them.

Gwenda Martin was the first to wake up, she had a habit of being the first to wake up on weekends. During the weekdays it would be Freddie, his alarm would wake him up. He would sit up in bed and cough his smoker's cough before the day began.

Gwenda was sitting at the table with a cup of black coffee in her hand. She took small sips from her mug, it was hot and steamy. Just how she liked it!

She had a dream last night, although there was a sense of realism to it that she couldn't help but not ignore. It interested her why she had a dream like this, at times she wondered what had caused her to have certain dreams. And this was one of those times. A dream that seemed to bend the physics of reality within her own mind. Crumbling those normal dreams and moulding them into something that seemed to not be monstrous. It was the only way she could describe it. She had done her normal bedtime routine, shower, brush her teeth, urinate and pray by her bed. Their bedroom was on the third floor of the farmhouse. Gwenda always believed that God was watching over her, she would kneel by her side of the bed and begin to pray. Thanking him for the life she had and the people she had in it.

Once she had climbed into bed and switched the light off by her bed and she attempted to drift off into a deep sleep. Her mind worked tirelessly as her eyes closed, for the next hour she remained awake. Her eyes did not feel heavy and she could not force herself to sleep, she could only hear the faint sound of her husband breathing. Along with the cold wind tapping on her bedroom window. Her side of the bed was by the window, she had drawn the curtains but she could still see the darkness through a small gap. The wind only grew more fierce as the hour progressed. She wasn't fond of it.

Gwenda had eventually allowed herself to nod off to sleep, her eyes shut slowly and her breathing slowed. She was consumed by the warmth of her husband and the blanket they were both tucked under. She brought her body towards him and began to cuddle him, he wrapped his large arms around her and rested his chin on her head. Although he was asleep he seemed to know what he was doing. Gwenda didn't know how much time had passed until she woke up again.

She was alone.

She was lying in the middle of the bed, her arms by her side and her head was on a slant. She was looking around her room, but she could only move her eyes. Her body felt heavy, she could not lift a single limb or even force herself upwards.

Gwenda's eyes darted around the room, nothing seemed to be out of place. Her dressing table was facing her and the wardrobe was pushed against the wall. She could see the door and the ceiling of her room, but what was it. Everything else was swallowed by the darkness. She could hear her heavy breathing, she knew what she was experiencing. She had gone through this before, Freddie had always been with her. He would hold her hand and tell her it was going to be okay and it was going to pass. It felt like hours before she could finally move again. And she would fear sleep.

But this time she was on her own with this one.

Gwenda saw something in the corner of the room, she didn't know what it was, she tried to force herself to remember what she had placed there.

Of course! The clothes on the chair!

Before bed, she had placed a pile of clothes to be ironed in the morning. Yet the dark silhouette began to move. The legs of the chair unfolded and stretched out like it had cramp. Two slender arms began to slowly unfold out of the mass of black.

Gwenda wanted to scream, she could not. She couldn't even make a muffling sound. No words or sounds came from her dry mouth.

The mass of black began to stand, it was now a dark bulking figure standing in the corner of her room. Its eyes burnt blood red and it's shoulder almost touched the ceiling. Gwenda felt it, her heart throbbing in her chest. Her skin began to form a sweaty layer on top. It stood there, just staring at her. She couldn't begin to imagine what this being was capable of doing to her, it's posture suggested a threat to her. If it wanted to it could crawl towards the bed and kill her!

Gwenda tried to cry out once more, cry out for Freddie. For anyone. Anyone to come to her and tell her that it wasn't really what she was seeing. To tell her what this being was was just nothing more than something that was in her fantasy.

Then it began to move towards her, the being did not move its legs. It was almost like it was floating towards her. If Gwenda could she would have screamed, get away from me! She could only lie there, her body helpless with her only eyes capable of moving. The being was slow with its movements, it flexed it's arms and spread its fingers wide. It was thin and its skin was seemed to have been pulled over its skeleton. Even with the being now at the end of her bed she could not make out its face save for those red burning eyes. It stopped and sat on the end of her bed. It turned it's head to face her, although it was dark and face showed no emotion. Gwenda swore she saw the being smile, it smiled and it showed no emotion still. Gwenda Martin was now nothing more than fear.

That was what Gwenda had experienced last night, and when she woke up she felt a sudden chill. The sleep paralysis still felt like a dream. Not a hallucination as it normally was. The scariest part of the dream was that the being did not stop smiling at her. It never spoke or even touched her. It sat on the end of her bed and smiled at her for what felt like hours upon end.

"Morning," said Freddie as he walked into the kitchen, he opened the teapot and started to make some tea.

"Morning darling," she sipped her coffee.

"You okay? Your pillow was covered in sweat this morning."

"I'm fine I just had a bad dream that's all," her cheek rested on her fist and she began to drink her coffee once more. She needed the caffeine to keep her awake for the busy day ahead.

"Really? That's weird. So did I."

"What was it?" she asked, she didn't care if she was honest.

"A dark figure. It was in our room. It towered over me

as I was stuck in your chair. It reached out for my neck, but I woke up after that."

"What? A tall dark figure?"

"Yeah, it was creepy. It wouldn't stop smiling as it reached towards me. Why?"

"I had a similar dream. Only it was smiling at the end of our bed."

"You was in the dream too, only you were in bed."

Gwenda's eyes went wide.

3

Thomas Martin woke up screaming, his hands wrapped around his head and he did nothing but scream. His hands got tighter and tighter and his vocal cords felt like they were going to snap like a guitar string. Michelle grabbed his shoulder and shook him, she cried, "Thomas! Thomas!"

He didn't respond, instead, he buried his face into his pillow and cried. He muffled the cry, he felt his eyes starting to tear up. Thomas didn't know what had started this, he wasn't the kind to get a headache that affected him like this.

It didn't take long for it to pass, but when it did the front of his head felt like a tight clamp was placed around it.

"Are you okay?" asked Michelle she was rubbing his cheek and pushing his hair out of his eyes.

"I'm fine. I just...I don't know what that was. My skin, it feels hot. I think I'm coming down with something," he held his throat. Thomas felt like he had swallowed a large ball of sand, his mouth felt dry and gritty, "I just need something to eat and drink. I should be fine after that."

"Are you sure? I can tell your dad that you're not feeling

well," said Michelle with a sense of concern in her tone. "No, don't tell my dad. It would just make things worse. Mum will start to mother me and probably send you home,"

Michelle stood up from the bed and ran her fingers through her messy hair.

"Don't be stupid Thomas. They won't send me home," she pulled down her nightdress and walked over to the window. She drew the curtains and peered outside, the morning was miserable.

"I don't think I will be able to get home anyway. The snow looks to be thick. It must have snowed heavy last night," she looked around the farm. The snow was fresh and undisturbed.

"Yeah, it was snowing before bed. I was expecting a blanket of the stuff to be honest," he was sitting up now. He put his elbows on his knees and rested his face in his palms, his cheeks felt sweaty and his black hair was plastered to his forehead.

"Michelle. Will you get me some water from the bathroom?" he took a glass from his bedside table. He took a glass up with him last night.

"Sure," she said as she took the glass from his weak grip. She left the room.

Thomas was thinking of what happened last night, the pair of them had climbed into his double bed and shared a kiss and cuddled each other. He was sure Michelle had drifted off before him. Thomas had found it rather hard to sleep last night, he felt warm and his skin felt prickly. Like he had fallen into a stinging nettle bush.

It must have been after one in the morning when his eyelids felt heavy, he snuggled his face into Michelle's shoulder and let himself drift off into his slumber. He was unaware of himself bringing Michelle closer to his chest, she pressed her head into his chest as she slept and gave a little cough.

Thomas Martin was soon dreaming, he was in his house outside of his mum and dad's room. The house was dark and there was not a single sound coming from inside or outside on the farm. He couldn't even hear his own breathing, his dream was in POV. As he headed downstairs he saw how the forest had started to grow within his home. Trees twisted around the stairs, it fused within the walls and long branches grew out of the walls like they had been glued there. Leaves were bushy and dark green and he had to push them out of his way as he descended down the stairs. He could now hear the howling wind and the banging of the front door like it was being opened and slammed shut again. Over and over again. Thomas gripped the bannister as he reached the ground floor, the front door was wide open exposing nothing but the darkness outside. And the darkness was breathing.

He walked across the hallway, hearing whispering coming from the cellar. The whispering of childlike voices, Thomas could not quite make out what they were saying. He had no choice but to ignore them, he walked to the front door. His hands trembling and his knees shaking. Thomas knew he should stop but there was something that was forcing him to keep moving. He couldn't quite put his finger on it. The temptation was getting too much!

He stepped out of the front door, the darkness growled at him. It moaned and he felt it begin to constrict around his wrists and throat. The darkness took a grip and dragged him into the air.

Michelle returned to him, in her hand she held the glass of water she handed it to him. Thomas took it from her and put it to his lips and took a drink. The feeling of the cold water in his mouth and going down his throat felt good for him.

"Thanks, I needed that," he put the empty glass back down on his bedside table with a sigh.

"I think mum is frying eggs," said Thomas as he sniffed the air. It was true, Gwenda was in the kitchen frying eggs and she had placed the bread in the toaster.

"She is. I heard her before asking if your dad wanted some. Are you hungry?"

"A little."

The two of them headed downstairs, all of the family, all apart from Heather and Agatha were sitting at the large table. Each of them tucking in for fresh fried eggs and buttered toast.

"Oh, you're awake! Come on its nearly half ten. Best get a move on!" said Freddie with a smile.

"Dad, I'm not feeling too good. I woke up in a sweat and with a tight headache," said Thomas as he sat down. Michelle sat beside him, she pushed her glasses up.

"Really? Oh. Well, it is the weekend anyway. Maybe you should take it easy. Have something to eat and see how you feel if you want lad," said Freddie as he poured himself a fresh mug of tea.

"He woke up screaming this morning," said Michelle. Gwenda stopped in her tracks as she placed two plates down on the table. One in front of Thomas and the other in front of Michelle, "Do you want anything Thomas? Any tablets or something" suggested Gwenda.

"No mum I'm okay. I'll just eat these eggs. If I don't get better I'll just go back to bed for the rest of the day. I

should be fine soon..." he let his words trail off.
"Are you feeling okay Michelle?" asked Gwenda.
"Oh yes, I'm fine. Thank you," replied Michelle with
politeness.
That was when it happened.
Thomas belched, he held his hand to his mouth. Then
vomit exploded from between his lips, it splattered on
the table. He had to turn his head away and vomited
onto the floor. It was pale yellow with tinges of white
floating around the edge of the puddle. It was the smell
that made him worse, Thomas hated the smell of vomit.
"Thomas!" cried Michelle, she grabbed his shoulders
and started to pat his back as hard as she could. His
younger siblings threw themselves away from the table.
Edna was gasping and looking away, Victor held his
hand to his mouth.
"Michelle take him upstairs please, here take this," said
Freddie as he handed the girl a bucket.
Michelle and Thomas began to limp up the stairs when
Gwenda said, "I am sorry Michelle. But can you tell the
girls to come down, please? But tell them to clean their
teeth first. Thank you."
Michelle nodded, she helped Thomas to the stairs but he
was fine to support himself. His face had gone pale, his
lips had turned blue and his eyes were watering.
"You'll be okay Thomas," she said as she wrapped her
hand around his waist. Then he snapped, "Don't touch
me!"

4

Agatha and Heather Martin had to share a bedroom, so
they had both awoken when Thomas screamed in his
room. Heather had woke up crying, Agatha hurried over

to her little sister and hushed her with love and empathy. She ran her fingers through her little sister's hair and told her it was all going to be okay and that Thomas had just stubbed his toe.

This was a lie, of course, Agatha had no idea what had happened to her brother.

She also had no idea what had happened out by the shooting range last night she knew she couldn't have imagined it. Those hands that reached out for her, those hands that had forced her to the floor. She knew it was real, there was no other explanation for what it could be. Agatha did not tell anyone in the house what had happened at the gun range. She knew her parents wouldn't believe her, she also knew that her siblings would laugh at her and call her pathetic. Agatha just went straight to her room, she forced herself onto her bed and began to sob. Her face was pressed into the pillow and she felt her heart thumping in her chest.

It was fear she felt when she saw those hands reach out and try to grab her. She didn't dream last night, her sleep was filled with emptiness and she would wake up every hour. Her eyes looking around her room. The clock ticked and the wind tapped on her windows. Heather snored loudly under her blankets.

Agatha tossed and turned wondering if she would ever get a good nights sleep. It never came.

Her eyes were sore and her eyelids felt heavy, even as she tossed and turned sleep did not come for Agatha Martin. Instead, she thought she would have to just lie on her mattress and wait for the sunrise.

Eventually, she managed to get two hours of sleep without waking. Her bedsheets were thin and took time for them to warm her up. When she managed to fall into a deep sleep, her family were plagued with nightmares. But Agatha was not. She woke up again after two hours and the time was 6:45 am.

She wanted to get some more sleep but her eyes would not close. She remained like this until she heard Thomas scream, she lifted her body and looked at her bedroom door. His scream sounded that of a sinister pain. Heather had woken up crying upon hearing her older brothers screams.

Agatha had stepped onto the landing and his scream was gone as fast as it had started. She heard Michelle and Thomas exchanging words in the bedroom. She couldn't hear what they were talking about, but she knew that Thomas was okay.

For now.

"I think he's okay Heather. He's just hurt himself that's all," whispered Agatha to her sister as she held her in her arms.

"Will he be okay?" said Heather with a sniff.

Agatha didn't know how to answer that question, she didn't know what had happened to Thomas.

"Yeah, I think he will be okay," she stroked Heather's hair softly.

The bedroom they shared was quite small, it fit two single beds and a large wardrobe and only a small set of drawers. Agatha hated it. The house was more than big enough for all of them to have their own rooms. The Brent brothers could have even moved into the house, but her dad didn't want that.

Agatha believed that her dad didn't trust the Brent brothers and she couldn't think why. They were both nice young men and were very helpful around the farm. Agatha's gaze caught the window, the glass had frosted over on the inside and outside of the glass panes. The wooden window ledge had become so damp the wood has started to rot and come apart near the edges. She withdrew the curtains after calming Heather down, the entire farm was engulfed in the fridged temperatures. Icicles had formed on the roof of the house and the border that went around the roof of the barn. She could almost smell the cold and how the coldness began to grow around the land itself. Agatha saw her breath in front of her as she breathed heavily.

She shivered.

Michelle knocked on the door and said, "Are you two decent?"

"Yeah, you can come in Michelle if you want," responded Agatha.

The beautiful girl came in, she closed the door behind her and ran her hands over her thighs to straighten her dress out.

"Your mum said you need to go downstairs but clean your teeth first," her voice sounded nervous.

"Okay, thank you, Michelle. How is Thomas? I heard him screaming this morning," Agatha had a hint of concern in her voice.

"He's fine. He just has the flu. I've put him to bed," she sucked on her bottom lip and put her left leg in front of her right leg so they were crossed.

There was a moment of silence between the three girls for a moment until Michelle broke it, "I should be getting back to Thomas. Bye," she hurried out of the room and left the door ajar.

Heather giggled a little and held her small hands to her cute button nose.

"Now you know Heather. Thomas is just fine. No need

to worry."

"Good!"

The two girls got up and went into the bathroom, it was a small bathroom on the second floor, the bath was pushed in the far right corner. And in front of them was the sink and the toilet was in the middle of the bath and the sink.

There was also a large window that was closed, but the cold had also frosted over the single glass pane. The house always got like this in the winter months. But this year something felt off.

The two girls took out their toothbrushes and began to clean their teeth. Agatha tried to turn on the cold water tap, but there was only the squeak of the handle as she twisted it. Her brow went up, there wasn't much she could do. She shrugged and the of them cleaned their teeth.

Heather asked, "What's wrong with the tap?"

"I don't know. I think the water has frozen in the pipes," she spat the peppermint paste into the sink.

Heather had finished first and skipped happily out of the bathroom. Leaving Agatha alone with her thoughts.

Agatha suddenly felt a cold breeze touch her bare legs. She looked around the room and saw that the window was wide open, the ice wind filled the room and made Agatha chatter her teeth. The cold wrapped around her like...cold hands. They seemed to grab her ankles and wrists, she suddenly found it hard to look away from the window. The whiteness was growing more and more fierce. As the cold became more bitter she felt the coldness wrap around her skull and go into her body. Her veins felt as if they were freezing within her body. She didn't say a word as her body slipped into the cold air outside.

5

Hugo Brent was sitting at the kitchen table. The morning air had left him feeling a little more awake. He woke up around 5:30 am in a shower of sweat. His pillowcase was covered in sweat and he had to go into the bathroom and cover his face with cold water. When he came out he sat in the kitchen drinking black coffee. But as soon as he made it he left it on the table for it go cold. He eventually decided to sip from the mug, but the taste seemed to change. It wasn't like drinking hot coffee. Cold coffee had a different feel to it. Well, it did to Hugo at least. He ran his fingers over he mug and was thinking about last night. He had a bad dream. A dream that had left him scarred. He could remember it as if it was a memory like it had occurred.

Sleep came to him quickly last night, himself and Richard spoke a little more before Richard decided to drink the bottle of rum he had hidden in his bedroom. Hugo stayed up until 11:30 pm and headed to his room. He could hear Richard, the man was crying and talking to himself. Hugo pressed his ear on the door and heard Richard say, "I'm sorry mum. I do love him. I know we don't get along too well. But I do love him. He might be a bit of a bastard at times. But I do love him, mum. Please. I want you to know that. I know I don't show him. No, just listen, please. I do love Hugo you know. He's my little brother at the end of the day. But I can't hate him you know. Yeah, yeah, yeah, yeah..."

Hugo presumed he was on the phone to his mum, but Richard was known to have conversations with himself and a brick wall. He got like that sometimes when he got drunk. Hugo went back into his bedroom and decided to climb under the sheets.

He let his head hit the pillow and he could still hear his older brother talking. He couldn't make out what he was saying and it wasn't too annoying.

Hugo then slipped off into sleep.

His eyes had closed and he tossed and turned without waking. He was warm in his bed and the cold air outside did not affect him.

Hugo couldn't put an exact time on when the nightmare had started but he guessed it must have been an hour or two after he closed his eyes.

In the dream he was in his cottage back in Orington, sitting in the back garden with his family. He had married Gwenda and the two of them had a child.

Richard was with his father at the BBQ making sure the food was cooked and prepared. Gwenda kept her hand on his lap, and the two of them shared a kiss.

He spoke with his family but when he tried to think what he spoke about it was more of a blur now. The memory that was fading, he had managed to remember the subject which they were discussing. It was regarding the farm and what had happened there. Hugo said something, but he more or less mouthed it.

Then the horror of the dream began. He only blinked and the entire world had changed. Everything was normal at first. Then he noticed how everyone he was with had vanished. There were no sounds made. Nothing. They just vanished.

Hugo stood up and looked around the garden, trying to figure out what was happening. As he got back to the patio he saw something. The curtain was shaking.

He looked closer.

Then faces appeared behind the glass, all of them pale and without emotion. Their eyes blank and their mouths slightly parted exposing their top row of teeth.
Hugo gasped and decided. The faces began to move as if they were balloons filled with helium. Some of them floated backwards and the others pressed on the glass. Hands then began to bang on the glass, each of them hitting the glass harder and harder. Then the heads spoke, they screamed, "HELP ME! SAVE ME! HUGO!" Hugo began to breathe heavily, he turned on his heels and began to run. His feet hammering into the grass but he found he was not going anywhere, the hands smashed the glass with force.
Hugo turned his head and the hands began to reach out for him. Long and thin, the fingers began to coil into his body. They started to fuse with his skin, as the fingers sank into him as if he was made of sand. They hurt and he started to scream and his skin began to bleed. Hugo was then snatched backwards, but he did not hit the window. He hit the wall, the bricks began to grow and bulge and his skin and body became part of the brickwork. He wanted to cry out for help, but the mixture covered his mouth and nose. Hugo was going to suffocate. His hands began to squirm and his legs start to kick, that all soon stopped as he sank deeper and deeper into the wall. Leaving just his eyes to see into the garden.
He was trapped.
As he waited he saw his parents, his brother and his daughter. Gwenda was not sat with Hugo now. She was sitting with Richard and she had her hand on his lap.
He tried to shout out but nothing happened.
Hugo was nothing more than eyes that would watch and

hear everything that was going on around him.
And he could do nothing about it.
Hugo had woken up after that and made himself the
coffee. As he sat at the table he finished the cold cup off
and then washed it in the sink.
Richard coughed and came out of his bedroom and he
muttered, "Morning..."
"Morning," said Hugo.
"You sound a little depressed tis morning. What's up
with thee now?" asked Richard as he started to make
some fresh coffee.
"Oh, it's nothing much. I just had a bad dream. Woke up
a little early for a Satday," he gave a little laugh at the
end of that.
Richard added a teaspoon of coffee into his mug along
with a splash of milk and let the kettle boil, "A
nightmare? Funny, so did I."
"Really?"
"Yeah, it was strange. Like I was in this cabin. Sitting at
the table. I was drinking and drinking. But I couldn't
stop. I was drinking some rum, as I poured it in me
mouth it kept coming. I couldn't even pull me hand
away."
The very thought made Hugo feel uneasy. The two
brothers had had a nightmare. Hugo then repeated his
nightmare only he changed Gwenda to some random
woman.
"Really? I bet it was the rum that did that," said
Richard.
"I didn't drink last night Rick," Hugo laughed as he sat
himself down on the armchair.
"Yes, you did. You came into my room and we had a
talk about family and shared the bottle of rum."

"Rick, honestly, I didn't drink last night. You wanted me to go to the Crossbow with you. But I said no. Then you came back in after the car had died. Then you took some rum into your room. You stupid fuck!"

"Wait. Wait. Wait! Hugo, I was sober when you came into my room and started drinking. I swear by it. I swear down on mum and dad's life me and you shared a bottle of rum."

Hugo knew that if he touched rum he would be ill, he didn't feel ill.

"I swear Rick, I didn't drink with you. I can't drink rum. It makes me feel bloated."

"Then who was I drinking with last night?"

The two brothers could only look at each other.

6

Victor Martin was sitting in the living room, he was tired and his legs felt a little sore. After he had eaten his breakfast he wanted to sit away from the table. He had finished eating it first and asked his mum if he could leave the table.

He sat alone, it was how he liked it. Victor heard his family chattering among themselves in the dining room. He heard forks tapping on plates and drinks being drunk. He would always sit at the table and have nothing to say, it was why he always finished his meals before anyone else. No one would ask him any questions of what his school life was like, or what his life was like anyway. Victor wasn't sure if they didn't care or if they just didn't think to ask him. But he cared.

Victor began to run his fingers through his hair before realising something, he poked his head into the dining room and looked around. His family were all seated and

still talking. Most of them dressed but Hester and
Heather were still in their nightgowns. He looked around
once more and said,
"Where's Agatha?" his voice sounded demanding but in
fact, he felt nervous.
Heather spoke in her sweet voice, "She's upstairs!"
egg and bacon exploded from her lips as she spoke.
Victor walked to the bottom of the stairs and shouted,
"Agatha!"
There was nothing but silence.
"Agatha!" shouted Edna as she joined her brother at the
stairs. The two of them looked at one another. Both of
them had a concerned look on their face, Freddie rose
from his chair and climbed up a few of the stairs, he
shouted, "Agatha! Darling! Your breakfast is ready!"
Again, there was silence.
Freddie turned his face to look at Gwenda, she sighed
and said, "She's probably messing around. Go and get
her Fred."
Freddie ran up the stairs as he continued to shout for his
daughter.
Victor and Edna went into the living room, the pair of
them sat themselves down on the couch.
They could hear their dad walking around upstairs.
His footsteps started to get louder as if he was
panicking. Freddie came down the stairs he almost threw
himself into the dining room and shouted,
"She isn't upstairs. I checked!"
For the first time, it set in, the dread. It was among each
and every one of them seated around the table. Sat in the
living room or standing in the hall.
"She's not upstairs? Are you sure?" asked Gwenda.
"I'm more than sure. I checked her room. I checked the

bathroom. I checked every room. She's not upstairs."

"Did she not come downstairs?" asked Freddie.

"No we would have seen her," stated Victor.

"Well where could she be?" said Gwenda as she looked around the room, "I'll look upstairs myself," she pushed past Freddie.

His large hand took a grip of her wrist and he said, "Do you not believe me?"

"I just need to be sure. I need to make myself sure."

"To be sure of what? That I'm not lying?"

"It's not that! You know how I get!" she pulled her arm free and ran up the stairs herself shouting her daughter's name.

The rest of the family were all drawn into the hallway. They looked up the stairs as they heard Gwenda's voice become more and more panicked.

Victor was close to the back and Edna had her hand on his shoulder. A few minutes felt like hours, the wait began to grow more and more tense. The siblings and dad all heard it when Gwenda shouted,

"Agatha! Where are you?"

They saw her walk down the stairs, her skin was pale and she was starting to shake a little.

She stopped at the base and said, "We need to find her. Look around the house. All of you. Get dressed. Go outside. Check the attic. Just look for her please,"

The siblings that were still in their nightclothes went upstairs, this included Victor.

He reached his bedroom and grabbed the handle, once he was inside he prayed that his little sister was sitting on his bed. But she wasn't.

Victor threw on the same clothes as yesterday and headed downstairs.

The house felt all empty as his siblings began to look outside, he heard footsteps on the porch. Victor put on some boots and a jacket before heading outside. It was colder than he thought he could feel the wind biting at his cheeks making them go numb. In the distance, he saw his father heading down towards the forest. Arthur was looking under the porch, Hester was by his side. But there was no sign of Edna or Heather.

Gwenda was heading towards the cabin where the Brent brothers slept. Or more or less lived.

Victor found himself wondering about the events that unfolded last night as he slept in his bed. He woke up, his skin soaked in sweat and he felt his heart thumping so hard in his chest he was scared it might burst out. Luckily his heart did not explode from his rib cage. He managed to calm himself down by throwing a handful of cold water from the bathroom sink on his face, he washed as much of the sweat from his body as he could. It was what he feared. The dream, he stayed in the lit bathroom for at least twenty minutes he would drink from the cold water tap or splash some on his face. All whilst thinking of the dream he had. It felt too powerful, it felt almost real.

Victor wasn't one for dreaming much as he slept in his bed, he had no trouble sleeping either. No matter how loud the night air was. Sleep would always come to him. He would go to bed with a glass of water and drink it through the night. Last night he finished most of the glass before reaching his bedroom door. He didn't think that much of it. He climbed into bed and he dropped off to sleep. Feeling the relaxing warmth of his blankets and pillow as he felt his eyes starting to close.

The dream must have started sometime after midnight, it

came fast and it came hard. Victor wished he didn't think of that dream, that dream that seemed to never end. That dream that was now coming true.

Victor felt it, it had already begun. Agatha was the first in his dream too. He held his breath, fearing who would be the next to die.

7

Freddie Martin was getting close to the tree line. His feet sank into the snow after each step he took, it crunched under his body weight. In the distance he would see the gun range, it was frosted over and the metal beams had become cold to touch.

But that was no concern of his at the moment, the only concern was finding Agatha. She couldn't just vanish clean off the farm, that was more than impossible. He wanted to find that little girl, find her and make sure she was alive and well. She had to be fine, there was no way she could be hurt. Or worst case scenario- dead.

No, he would not think of such things. Agatha was alive and well, it was just a question of where she currently was. She couldn't have gone far. She was only wearing her nightgown. Unless she had gotten dressed and gone for an early morning walk, she usually did. Most of the others had gone off in pairs. It was only Freddie who was alone in this situation. It was how he wanted it if he was honest. If he found her before anyone else he would not be mad with her, he would just tell her to not wander off ever again.

He got thinking about the past again.

Thinking of the past with little Agatha. She hated guns when they went hunting in the forest, she would always ask for something quieter. And something that didn't hurt your hands as much as a rifle. That was when Freddie had the bright idea of buying a crossbow. It was in her bedroom at this moment in time. A wooden crossbow, with the stock of that, resembled a rifle. The bolts were large black things with white fletchers. But it was the arrow that was deadly, it was barbed and powerful. It could cause a great deal of damage if one was to get a good shot with it. He took her and only her into the forest one summers morning, the pair of them sat peacefully behind a collapsed tree. They only had the crossbow with them, it was leaning on the trunk of the tree as the two of them exchanged conversation. It was a bright conversation, Freddie couldn't recall the exact words but it was about their life. And how much she loved him, he would never forget a certain line she said to him. That line would stay with him forever, until his dying day.

She said, "You know what dad. Even if we don't catch something. Even if I can't take a shot of this crossbow. I am glad that I could spend some time with you. Just me and you. I love you," she rested her head on his shoulder then. Her hair touching his cheek and neck, he was speechless. He had never had any of his children say that to him! Sometimes their actions said it, but it was also nice to hear it now and then.

They did catch something that day. Freddie heard something walk slowly in the trees, he lifted his head and a deer strolled across the floor. It bowed it's head to chew on the patches of grass that grew around the base of the trees. Freddie gestured for Agatha to take aim and she did, she lifted the crossbow and got ready to fire. She pulled the trigger with a light squeeze of her finger, although it wasn't as powerful as a rifle she felt the kick.

The bolt struck the deer in its neck, penetrating its throat, knocking the animal down on its side. It let out a cry and hit the floor with a heavy thud, a flock of birds flew away in the distance.

Agatha cheered.

She jumped over the tree and ran over to the deer, crossbow still in hand, and stopped near its body. The animal was still alive, it was moaning in pain. Blood trickled down its neck and out of its mouth. Agatha lifted her hand to her mouth and knelt by its side. She pressed her hand on its face and began to cry. Freddie walked over and placed his hand on her shoulder and said, "I was like that. My first kill. It was awful. Your granddad shouted at me to open fire, I pulled the trigger. My eyes sore with tears. I missed the head. Hit the animal in its body. It ran away. I was forced to follow the trail of blood, not the best decision I ever made you know. I found the deer not long after, he was on his side. Bleeding to death. My dad told me to cut its throat to end it's suffering. I didn't want to harm it any more. I couldn't bring myself to do it. But my dad did, he used the rifle. Put a bullet in its head. I eventually learned that sometimes we have to do things that we don't want to do. I won't make you do it, Aggie."

She never harmed that deer on that day, Freddie used his hunting knife to slash its throat. The deer was cooked and eaten over the course of one week. Some of it was even sold in Orington.

Freddie started his descent down the hill to the forest, it was covered in snow and very slippy. Tree roots wrestled their way through the hard ground and seemed to have become frozen in place.

He almost slipped when he reached the bottom of the

hill, he used a tree for support. When he regained his balance he shouted, "Agatha!"

All Freddie could hear was his panic-filled breathing. It was frozen after it came out of his mouth, he could see it. Only for a few seconds before it disappeared. Freddie Martin decided it would be best to go a little into the forest and then return to the farmhouse. He hoped to find his little girl alive and well. It was the only thing he hoped for. But as a parent, he began to think of the worst possible outcome for his daughter. She could be severely injured for all he knew. Then something hit him. He realised there weren't any tracks in the snow. Nothing apart from his footprints, that was behind him. He took a few steps forward, then something on a tree disturbed him. It was something that made him catch his own words in his throat, his hands trembled. Not from the cold. But from the fear that began to coil around his body like a python. On one of the large trees with black oak and long branches were various symbols. Markings that didn't seem to be some random shapes carved into the wood. From the branches, there was string and attached to them were feathers. They blew gracefully in the wind, but on the tree, it's a self made Freddie want to vomit. It splattered from his mouth and onto the snow staining it a light orange colour and a mixture of brown. His mouth tasted bitter and sour.

Something then dripped on his forehead, he lifted his hand and felt his skin. When he looked at his fingers he saw red. His eyes looked up and saw something in the trees. It didn't seem like it was part of the forest.

That was when he saw it, the bare feet and the nightgown. He had to get closer. He approached what looked like a body and peered up through the mangled branches and staring back at him was a face, a face that looked all too familiar to him. Then he saw the eyes, blank marbles and the face was suffused with blood and her lips were blue. He managed to force a word out of his lips, "Agatha..."

She was twisted and tangled in the branches, her face stared coldly and her mouth was open wide, her body must have been at least 30ft in the air.

Freddie's knees suddenly felt weak, they began to shake and touch each other. His entire body became numb and he collapsed into the snow, hearing nothing but static.

His legs began to kick uncontrollably, his arms began to push the snow away as they shook around out of his control.

It's started. It's coming. It will consume you all.

Consume you like the fridged snowfall.

Your weakness is yourself.

He began to vomit again, this time it was only bile.

His eyes went bloodshot and his nails dug into the earth, his legs continued to kick over and over again. He felt pain in his spine and his muscles started to ache as if someone had put glass under his skin.

Endless pain...

Endless suffering...

Freddie Martin stopped moving.

He was unconscious.

8

Gwenda peered around the side of the barn, she sighed when she discovered Agatha was not there.

She pressed her head on the barn and punched the wooden boards as hard as she could. She had told her children to look everywhere. Her husband had suggested the forest and had made his way to the treeline. Gwenda was having no luck.

She hoped someone would find her soon. To end this continuous feeling of dread and wondering of the whereabouts of Aggie.

As she pressed her back on the barn she checked her hand, it was bruised near the knuckles and looked to be sore. She ran her fingers over it, the bruise started to tingle and hurt.

"Having no luck?" came a familiar voice.

She looked upwards and saw Richard Brent walking towards her with his younger brother both of them dressed for the cold weather.

"No! If I was having luck Richard I would have found her by now!" she snapped at him.

Richard took a step back and lifted his hands before saying, "I'm sorry Gwenda. I'm just trying to-"

She interrupted him politely, "I know. I know. I'm sorry Richard. I'm just stressed out with the whole situation."

"It's okay. I'll go and look near the porch with Edna and Victor," he walked away towards the farmhouse. His hands tucked into his pockets and his head pointed downwards.

Hugo Brent remained with Gwenda.

"We'll find her you know," he said as he lit a cigarette.

"I thought you quit smoking?" asked Gwenda.

"I have the odd one every now and again. I still get the urge shall we say."

"I could do with one right around now. I stopped smoking after I gave birth to Victor. I didn't want to harm my children with what I was doing. If anything happened to them whilst I was smoking. I would never forgive myself," she placed her face into her palms.

"ere," Gwenda lifted her head and Hugo was holding a rolled cigarette, he was offering it to her.

"I shouldn't," she shook her head.

"It's only one. It might calm you down. It does the job for me you know. I know this will work me," said Hugo as he blew smoke out of his mouth.

"No. I shouldn't have one."

"You have never refused anything from me Gwenda," his lips formed a smile. A handsome smile.

"That was a long time ago, and you know it Hugo."

"It was only a few years ago."

"I have moved on from what we had those years ago Hugo. I was in some dark times, you were my anti-depression medication. I needed you. But not now. You are a nice man Hugo. But please. Just pretend what happened didn't. Please. For me?"

He put his cigarette back in the packet and nodded with agreement.

"Yeah. Okay. I understand."

It was true with what she was saying. Gwenda had fallen into a deep depression around five years ago, it was her darkness. And it was eating away at any happiness she had with her family, but more of Freddie. She loved him. He loved her. But their marriage was slowly falling apart, it was due to the death of one of her children. She had a boy named Toby. He was born a year after Victor. He was just nine years old when he died.

The combine harvester was going through the fields of wheat on the far top right of the farm. And young Toby was playing by the wheat.

It all happened at once, the boy screamed out in pain and Freddie didn't even notice until a streak of blood splashed across the window. He stopped the combine immediately and ran to the front. He saw Toby, he was mangled and twisted in the blades. But he was still alive. His entire left arm and leg were crushed and torn apart. His neck had a shard of metal slicing through it. Toby didn't have much time left alive, he couldn't even reach out to his dad before he died. His body became limp and blood bubbled from his lips as he died. His skin was pale and his lips had turned blue.

Freddie knelt by his dead son and screamed.

The family had never been the same since. Freddie had found comfort in the bottle. Whilst Gwenda had found comfort in Hugo Brent. The pair of them spoke in his cabin and got along really well.

Then it happened...

No, she didn't want to think of what she had done with him, it was all a big mistake and nothing more. It was something she didn't want to talk about. Nor think about.

"Maybe you need to calm down another way," he said as he placed a hand on her waist.

"I just want to find my daughter at this moment in time Hugo. Being in bed with you has not crossed my mind for the past five years thank you."

"Really? You haven't craved me once? You haven't found your fingers running over your clit. Thinking it's my hand rubbing on you," his lips formed that handsome smile once more.

"No Hue. I have not done that. What I did to you was wrong. I shouldn't have done it to you. You were just a young man. I was just desperate for love and affection and you-"

"-I gave it to ya."

"You did. I am grateful for what you did for me. I cannot

thank you enough for what you did for me. But it's over. You need to understand that. Okay?" She started to walk past him but his hand took a grip of hers.

"What about once more? For old times sake? I can't help it Gwenda. I can't help but think of you. God, you make me...God, I can't even word how you make me feel. I just feel great thinking about you."

His hand began to slip into her coat, it worked it's way to her breasts and he began to fondle with her.

She didn't resist.

He started to kiss her, at first she didn't respond.

But then she grabbed the back of his head and started to kiss him back, her tongue in his mouth and her hand grabbing his crotch.

"In the barn," she said.

The pair of them went inside the barn through the back door.

Once they were inside she took him upstairs and into a small room that was surprisingly warm.

She took off her jacket and he took off his.

Before either of them knew it they were both completely nude, she felt his penis poke in between her thighs. She kept her hands on his torso and he did the same. He kissed her neck and was tempted to give her a love bite but stopped himself, it was only a one-off!

"Are you sure?" he said.

"I am," she replied with a smile.

They continued to kiss for a while until she was on her back. Pressed against some old bedsheets and pillows, he kissed her body down to her thighs and licked from her bellybutton to her neck. She moaned and he panted. Hugo ran his fingers over her stomach then down to her thighs, he brushed across her skin with soft strokes and with passion. He wanted to be gentle with her, just like he used to be.

"Oh Hugo," she ran her fingers through his long hair and she forced his head between her breasts.

He kissed her neck and she said, "You can put it in now if you want."

He nodded and she guided him in between her wet legs.

9

The search party had continued all morning. And all Heather Martin could do was sit in the house and wait for them to come back. She had no idea what had happened but she was keen on finding out. From what she could gather from her mummy and daddy Agatha was not in the house. But most of them wasn't in the house most of the time, they were outside with the animals on the grass or in the big wooden building across from the house. Even as a four year she could register that there was something wrong with her parents, they seemed angry but upset at the same time. She couldn't quite figure it out. Her mummy had told her to stay inside the house where it was warm, they told her if she needed anything she was to call for Edna.

Edna was at the front of the house with Victor. Heather had sat on the couch and watched television. But the screen went all weird and full of lines and made a crackling sound. It eventually cut to black and she was forced to draw with crayons on the coffee table. The girl was on her knees at the table, her small hand held a red crayon as she drew with it. She drew some faces with her childish attitude. One eye bigger than the other and a mouth that was a scribble on the page.

She got bored with drawing and decided to resort to

something a little more interesting. Heather wanted to go outside. The very idea was in her head all morning, she wanted to go out in the snow and build snowmen and make snow angels.

She wanted to be an angel, they were things of beauty. She had seen pictures in the books, long golden hair with long silk dresses and above their lock of hair. Was a beautiful halo that glowed like the sun. Sometimes they held a harp and that was what Heather wanted, to be beautiful with large wings of feathers that fluttered as graceful as a butterfly.

Her mummy had told her on numerous occasions that she was an angel! But then again she also said that her dead grandparents were also angels, flying through the clouds of heaven. Watching over their granddaughter. Every Christmas the girl waited for angels to fly into her garden and sprinkle their magic across the floor. Every morning of Christmas day she would go outside first and look for angel magic. She would find it, but it was part of the snow now. The way it sparkled like thousands and thousands of diamonds crusted into the ice.

Her mummy had always that Agatha was also an angel, had Agatha flew away? Heather hoped she didn't. She loved Agatha. She loved all of her brothers and sisters but Agatha was her favourite.

Maybe when she cleaned her teeth she flew out of the bathroom window, daddy said it was left open.

It made sense!

Yes, that is what happened to Agatha, she flew away! Heather wished she could fly away, but maybe she wasn't ready yet. Agatha was 11 years old and Heather was only 4 years old. There was a difference in their ages.

Lucy strolled into the living room, she was wagging her tail and her mouth was open. Heather stroked the dog and let the dog lick her cheeks, Stella soon strolled in too and Sam soon followed. The three dogs surrounded Heather and their tails were wagging quickly, it would be like a whip if it was to strike the frail girl. She laughed as they licked her and began to get close to her. Heather wrapped her arms around the dog and pulled Lucy forward, she laughed louder and kissed the dog on her cheek. Lucy kissed her back with a sloppy tongue. The dogs began to force Heather down and lick her quickly as if they were tasting her skin.
Heather laughed.
Then the front door opened, "Heather?"
It was Edna, the girl came into the living room and smiled at the sight. She shooed the dogs away and helped Heather to her feet. Edna was wrapped up warm, she sore mittens, a scarf, boots and a woolly hat that her mother had knitted for her.
"Did you find Aga fa?" said Heather as she threw her body onto the sofa. She bounced a little before landing down softly.
"No, not yet Heather. We will find her, so don't go worrying about her okay?"
"She will be okay. I think she flew away! Like an angel. Mummy always said she was an angel!"
Even though Heather had a sweet warm smile plastered on those small lips Edna felt as if she was going to tear up. She had to look away before she said, "Yeah. Maybe. But I think mummy and daddy would like it if she was here. Don't you?"
"Yes. I would love it if she was here," she threw her arms into the air. Then she said, "Can I help find her?"

Edna looked at Heather with an expression of worry, she shook her head and said, "No Heather. It's too cold outside. Look my nose has gone all red from the cold!" It was true, even when Edna had opened the front door she felt the air turn cold almost instantaneously. It was unnaturally cold outside today, all of the windows had become glazed with ice. Icicles had formed around the roof of the porch and the front door was frozen shut, it took her dad and Victor to pry it open. She heard the ice crack and snap as the door was flung open.

"How cold is it?" asked Heather as she tried to look out of the window.

"Very. You remember the door this morning, don't you? It was frozen shut!"

"Oh my!" said Heather.

That was her favourite expression to use these days, Oh my! She used it a lot when something bad was happening, or she knew something bad was going to happen.

"Yeah, it's really cold outside. It's why I'm all bundled up," she laughed a little. If it was to ease the pain of her missing sister or if it was to make Heather understand how cold it was. She didn't know. Edna would sometimes find herself repeating words or phrases to make sure Heather fully understood what she was saying. She was only a little girl at the end of the day.

"I'm going to go and see if I can find Agatha. Stay here with the dogs okay?"

"Okay!"

Edna began to leave the living room, when she looked back she saw that small baby face staring at her. Her large eyes smiling and those lips forming a little grin. She was a child in a world filled with adults. She slipped out of the front door. A cold chill of wind blew into the living room and made Heather shiver.

She looked out of the window and could see Edna walk across the porch and towards Victor. The two of them were heading towards the old well. Mummy told Heather to not go near there, the stones were weak and the water was really cold. Especially in winter. Sometimes it would freeze over creating an icy pit within. Heather had never gone near it, the well made her feel a little uneasy.

She missed Agatha.

This morning had been a little too eventful. Her older brother, Thomas, had fallen ill and there was talk of strange things in dreams. Heather also had a dream, she dreamt of a coldness.

A cold tube of stones, she was falling through it. Feeling something hit her hard in the body, and something splashed up into her face. When she stood up she realised where she was.

...at the bottom of the well.

And it was getting smaller and smaller!

She began to cry and scream feeling how tight it was becoming and how terrifying it was for her.

She felt her hands touch the cobble blocks used to construct the design of the well. And then a cold clammy hand wrapped around her face and stopped her from breathing.

Heather woke up in her bedroom with sweat beads all over her face, her hair was almost glued to her cheeks and forehead. She had to rinse her face was cold water to cool herself down. After that, she sat in her room and cried, Agatha was there to provide comfort and made her feel better. It was all in her head and nothing more.

Things you made up could not hurt you, could they? Heather soon got an idea, she wanted to help find Agatha. She couldn't have gone very far could she? Maybe she was playing hide and seek and didn't want to tell anyone where she was hiding. It made sense for her to not say anything, it was the rules of the game after all. Heather walked into the hallway and past the door to the cellar.

She was always told to never go down there, it was a dangerous place as it was cold and filled with tools that daddy had. She came to the coat rack and pulled down her coat. Her woolly hat and gloves came with it. She removed her shoes and slipped on some white Wellington boots. Once she buttoned up her coat she opened the front door. She felt the coldness grab her as soon as the door swung open.

The snow was falling softly and she heard the whip of the wind followed by someone shouting, "Agatha! Where are you?" it sounded like Victor.

Heather looked around the farm, the Brent cabin was still and dead. Agatha wouldn't be hiding there, she thought. She looked around the farm again and saw the barn. Heather ran down the stairs to the porch and ran across towards the barn. It was a quiet place. No sounds from the outside, not even the horses or goats. She barely heard a thing. So far at least.

She entered the barn through the back, once she was inside it suddenly felt a little warmer. The sound of horses was clear and-

-another sound?

It didn't sound like any farm animal she had heard before, it was heavy and there was almost a slapping sound to it. She looked around the barn, there was still no sign of Agatha. She sighed and heard someone laughing upstairs and then someone said, "Shh..." Heather then started to work her way up the small set of stairs to the second floor on the barn. She was quiet and almost completely silent. She reached the door to the small room and slowly went on her tiptoes to look inside.

There was a pile of sheets and removed clothing littering the floor. She then saw two people, one was on top of the other and they were panting heavily, she saw the top one more. It was a man, his face was buried in the chest of the woman. His hands ran over her body, he was hurting her!

She felt nervous and decided she was going to save the woman. She opened the door and saw who the woman was, it was her mummy!

Heather shouted, "Stop hurting my mummy!"

They turned around and looked into her eyes.

It was Hugo!

Heather let out a cry and heard her mummy cry, "Heather! Don't look! Mummy and Hugo were just fighting!"

Heather was sick with fright, she turned on her heels but her snow-covered boots didn't let her get far. She slipped and skidded, her body struck the wooden railing.

It snapped.

Her body flew through the air and she hit the concrete floor with a heavy thud. The last thing she remembered was darkness and the sound of an egg cracking on the rim of a stone dish.

10

"Oh no. Oh no. Oh God! Oh shit!" cried Gwenda Martin, she stood up and quickly pulled her dress down.

Once she got out of the room she ran to the railing. The wooden plank had snapped in two and caused Heather to fall at least a few feet. She saw her daughter. Lying on her back, her eyes closed and blood was coming out of her nose. Gwenda quickly descended the stairs and ran to her daughter. Once she reached her she lifted her into the air and slapped her gently on the face.

"Come on. Come one. You stupid girl!" screamed Gwenda. That got the attention of Richard Brent.

He slowly opened the door and said, "What's happened?"

As soon as he saw Gwenda holding Heather's body he said, "Oh God!" he ran over to them and knelt beside them. His hand ran over Heather's forehead and he felt for a pulse, his finger ran under her nose, "She's alive. What happened?"

"She fell!"

"Shit. I think she'll be okay. But take her into Orington!"

Gwenda nodded and picked up Heather, she was light for her age. Her hair hung freely around her face as Gwenda almost dashed out of the barn.

Once she left Richard looked up and saw Hugo standing on the second floor looking down. His shirt was off.

"What have you been doing?"

"Nothing," said Hugo as he pulled himself back inside the small room.

"Have you been going at it again?" asked Richard as he strolled to the base of the small stairs.

Hugo didn't reply. Instead, he threw on his clothes, he slipped on his shirt and jumper before fixing himself by looking in the window.

"Hugo? I asked you a question," continued Richard as he began to climb up the stairs.

"I know you did!"

"Well answer it will ya!" even Hugo could sense the anger in his brother's voice.

"We was. Yes. Are you happy?"

"No! I thought you stopped all that," Richard was blocking the way to the stairs and even the door at the far end of the platform.

"Well, I did. But I've been craving her lately. I don't know what it is. But it's almost like an urge. I think I love her!"

"You need to stop it. She's your bosses wife. If you keep sleeping with her, he will find out you know. He's not stupid Freddie," said Richard with confidence.

"He is Rick. I've been fucking her for the past five years. He didn't even bat an eye. It just goes to show that his life is this farm. Not his beautiful wife or his children. It's this sorry excuse for a farm."

"What's wrong with you? This isn't you!"

"And your point is? Listen, Rick, if you can fuck a woman who is perfect in every way. You would. So don't bullshit me."

"I'm not. Wait. Five years?"

"Yeah, five years. It was when Toby died. The pair of them got depressed. I was like her medicine."

"Was you protected?"

"I don't know. Maybe a few times, why?"

"Have you not considered the consequences of your actions?"

"It's not like I have HIV or anything."

"I'm not on about that!" shouted Richard as Hugo finally decided to leave the room. He looked like he did this morning. But the smell of sex was near him.

"What are you...Oh shut up. I always make sure I pull

80

out."

"Really? You mean every time!"

"What is this? Are you jealous lover boy?" said Hugo with that handsome smile once more.

"You are really winding me up now Hugo. You have to stop sleeping with her! She's just lusting after you! And you are the same!"

"Well you should love yourself," Hugo winked at his brother.

"I swear I'm going to punch you if you keep this up!"

"Calm down Richard," said Hugo as he got closer. Richard felt his hands clamp hard into fists, he looked at his brother's pretty face and said, "You deserve this Hugo! You really do!"

Richard swung upwards at his younger brother, he felt his fist collide with Hugo's chin and he heard something crack.

Hugo grunted loudly and held his chin as he pulled himself backwards. Feeling the force of the fist collide with him and he landed on his buttocks. Hugo held his chin and cried, "You bastard!"

Hugo jumped up and kicked his brother hard in the knee causing him to slip and go down on that knee. Hugo then kneed Richard in the face, breaking his nose and causing it to bleed. As he was about to punch him again Richard charged at him, he tackled him down on the floor and they heard the wood creak. Hugo punched his brother, each fist lifted and slammed hard into Richard's face. Feeling his hard skull with every hit, his skin was becoming more and more wet with every hit.

When Hugo stood up he grunted and rubbed his hands, his knuckles were swollen and red. Not from the force of punching Richard but the blood from Richard's lip, nose and brow. Richard lay on his back. Weak from the beating Hugo had given him.

"Don't tell me how to live my life!" said Hugo.

Richard rolled over onto his side, spitting blood and teeth out of his mouth. His face was badly bruised and swollen.

"I...I was..." Richard could not finish his sentence. Instead, he let out a loud groan.

Hugo grinned and turned on his heels, he began to walk down the stairs when he heard Richard scream. It wasn't like the scream of pain, it was more like the scream of fear. Hugo went back up on the platform and looked at Richard. He was running towards Hugo, his left eye was wide open and filled with fear, "Run! Arghh!"

Richard suddenly fell onto his side, his left leg was twisted and broken. He cried out with tears streaming down his cheeks, Hugo saw it!

"Oh god!" he screamed, he reached out for Richard. But he was dragged across the floor, his nails digging into the wood. When Richard screaming stopped Hugo saw it move across the wall. It ran towards him with-

Hugo made a horrible sound in his throat, blood bubbled from the corner of his lip and it pumped down his chest from the new slash deep in his throat. He heard it splash onto the floor in large amounts. The smell was thick in the air. His hands reached up towards it, soaking his hands in red. It was like they had been dipped into a bucket of red paint.

The last thing Hugo Brent remembered was not a sexual thought of Gwenda Martin or any empathy for the beating he gave to Richard Brent. No. His final thought was of sadness and strong fear. As his eyes saw his feet his mind soon went dead.

11

When Gwenda Martin reached the house her children helped her with Heather, the three dogs were running around them. Sniffing and curious with what was happening with their master. Victor quickly moved the dogs away from his mum.

"Here, put her here," said Gwenda as herself and Edna lowered Heather onto the sofa she was bouncing on a few moments ago.

Once she was on the couch Gwenda used some blankets that were thrown over the back of the sofa, to make sure Heather was comfortable.

"She needs a doctor. Victor go and call for them. Edna get the medical box. Hurry both of you!" the two siblings quickly rushed into the kitchen. Victor pulled the phone from the wall and quickly dialled the number for the Orington doctor. The phone rang.

Edna pulled open a chest of drawers and quickly looked through them, she moved plastic tubs, small towels and various piles of papers. When she reached out to the back of the drawer she found the small green box. She pulled it upwards and unclipped it, inside was various bottles of medication and capsules. There was even a syringe and next to it was a small bottle titled: MORPHINE.

Edna picked up the medical tape and the bandages. She left the kitchen quickly and headed back into the living room.

Victor remained in the kitchen on the phone. Then the phone ceased to ring out, he quickly dialled the number again and made sure it was correct. But the dial tone wasn't there. He placed the phone back on the hook. Victor entered the living room, his mum was wrapping a bandage around Heather's little skull.

"It's cracked," said Gwenda as she pulled her bloody palm away from the back of Heather's head, "Victor are the doctors on their way?"

Victor could see various emotions going on with his mum at the moment. But the biggest one was probably fear. Fearing that her daughter may die.

"No. The phone. It doesn't work. It was ringing then it went dead," his voice trembled.

"What? No, it can't be. Edna, please check for me."

Edna left and returned after a moment she shook her head and said, "He's right. It doesn't even have a dial tone. I checked the wire. It's not snapped or anything," Gwenda lifted her head and looked at her two children, "Where's your dad?"

"He's looking for Agatha in the forest," said Edna.

Since having sex with Hugo and carrying Heather inside she forgot about Agatha. She forgot about the real reason why she was even outside in the first place. Gwenda placed her head in her hands and began to sob.

"Agatha..." she whimpered.

"He will find her mum. We looked all over the farm. She's nowhere to be seen. Was there nothing in the barn?" said Victor.

Gwenda shook her head.

"Dad should be back soon," said Edna.

"What do you know!" shouted Gwenda, "How will you know when he comes back?" her tone had changed and it took Edna back a little.

"I'm sorry I was just saying," her words trembled.

Gwenda sat herself down next to Heather, the three dogs had curled themselves up and lay down in front of the fire. The flames crackled and the wood continued to burn.

Edna left the living and sat herself down in the dining room.

Victor sat in the armchair, he didn't know what else he could do. There was nothing else he could do really. Nothing but wait.

12

His mind was plunged into a pit of torture and the great nothing. Once soft sounds had turned into the stuff of nightmares. As cold fingers wrapped around the trees and slowly worked their way towards him, he felt a dozen eyes watching him. Like a constant stalker. But when he looked up there was nothing there. Just a sky of blackness. Not a single star was in sight, he ran his hands through his hair and looked up the hill. Didn't I run deeper into the woods? He thought as he began to climb the hill. It was steep and it scared him. Each step he had to make sure his feet were wedged into the ground. The steep then started to change, from mud and snow to wood and carpet. It was turning into stairs, the same stairs that were in his house!

What was happening?

The hill was soon transformed into a monstrous mixture of wooden floorboards and hardened mud as it crunched under his boots. The smell remained, the smell of winter. And the air was cold, his body began to shiver. Freddie continued his long walk up the stairs. He was sure it took him no more than five seconds to reach the second floor of the farmhouse. But this time. Things were different. They felt off. They felt the same yet different in ways that he could not describe with words in the English language.

Was this another dream? Another dream that would wake him up? What happened before his mind was darkness?

Agatha!

He had seen her, that cold pale as she hung in the branches of the tree, horrific symbols carved into the bark from the branches, feathers floating softly on the string and the smell of blood in the air. What was happening?

He had all these questions yet not a single answer came. His body began to feel weak, his hands trembled as he held onto the bannister. His knees shook and he felt his jaw rocking from side to side. Freddie Martin felt something, not something touching him. He felt an emotion or a more human instinct to survive. He ducked his head and went on his knees on the stairs, his joints felt heavy. All of them, he didn't want to look up. He swore he felt something jump over the top of him.

And something did.

It was there, at the top of the stairs, he saw its head and it was peaking over the top step. Its eyes were that of hollow and its head was skinless. Exposing the twisted bone beneath, it was cracked as if struck by something with force and all the creature did was stare.

It stared as if it was staring deep into his body.

Freddie lifted his head and felt the cold shiver run down his spine. Like countless fingers brushing over his back. The being, what was it? What did it want with him? What did it want with his family? The being pulled itself away, and a part of him wanted to turn away and run out of the house. But another part, it was more curious and it had a stronger amount of motivation. He pulled himself on his feet and began to walk up towards the landing.

Every step he took.
Every breath he made.
Every heartbeat.
Every time he moved he felt an insane amount of fear.
Freddie soon reached the landing, his house had become
part of the forest, the wooden floorboards were now
littered with snow. Trees grew out of the wall as if they
were part of a décor.
The being was there, sitting in the corner of the hallway,
it's head pointed downwards with its knees tucked under
its chin.
"What are you?" said Freddie.
"I am you. I am the farm. I am the world. I am the
universe. I am a being of superior status."
But when the being turned to face Freddie he felt like his
body was frozen into place. Those eyes!
Oh God, Those EYES!
It was at that exact moment that Freddie Martin had
finally awoken. But he was not in the same position as
he was when he fainted. He was now wearing only his t-
shirt and underwear. His feet were tucked under his
buttocks and his hands were in the praying position.

13

Freddie pulled himself away from the tree, he was
shivering and his hands had turned red from the cold. He
wrapped his arms around his body and looked around
for his clothes. He quickly slipped his jeans on, then his
socks and finally his boots. The cold was becoming
unbearable and he felt extremely weak. He looked back
up at the tree and was horrified by how it looked.
It looked completely different from the other trees, it
was tall and the bark was black. All possible life seemed

to avoid it, the branches twisting like broken fingers and the trunk looked like a dead arm rising from the snow. And the symbols that were carved into the bark seemed to be that of Satanism, and Freddie was worshipping it! He was still on the floor when he was fully clothed, his skin was cold and he continued to shiver, his hands felt numb and he was losing the sense of feeling in his fingertips, please don't be frostbite! He thought.

Once he was on his feet he had a sudden urge to vomit, and he did. It splattered out of his mouth and the snow changed colour where it struck.

Freddie held his mouth and leaned against the tree, that was when he felt something. It wasn't bark or snow or anything that you might put in a forest. It felt soft and wet when he looked up he saw-

"Toby?"

Toby Martin was standing in front of him, his clothing was torn and bloody. But his face, oh god his face. The skin was torn clean from the bone muscle tissue was exposed as was his brain. Freddie was taken back when the combine tore through Toby's body and his scream was heard. Freddie quickly climbed out and saw Toby, his body was twisted and mangled in the blades.

His skin was tangled in the blades and Freddie knelt by his son, he held him as he was dying. Blood pumped from the open wounds and Freddie felt his heart stop beating for a split second. He held the boy and his shirt and jeans were soaked with blood, Freddie held Toby's head and said, "Shhh, it's okay. I'm here."

Toby's eye rolled to the side and looked into Freddie's, then it rolled back. The eyelid closed and he died right there and then. Freddie burst into tears at that moment. Toby stood still not speaking mainly because his throat had ripped open and his tongue was now in his windpipe. He stood staring with one pulverised eye, egg white like fluid mixing with the blood and the other was fine and staring deep into Freddie.

"Toby? Good god. You're alive!"

Toby didn't respond, instead, he reached out and pointed towards the direction where the hill was. He opened his mouth and although he didn't speak Freddie heard it inside his head, "Barn. Barn."

Freddie pulled himself backwards, Toby stood still. That was when Freddie noticed it, his right arm. It was part of the tree the bark had grown around it and was continuing to pull him towards the trunk.

"Toby? How?" asked Freddie.

Toby twisted himself and did a strange move, his arm flexed outwards and his head snapped to the side. Most of the left side of his body had been torn apart from the blades of the combine. Each one ripping through his flesh and plucking him apart like a feathered chicken. Each time the blade sank into him he would try to scream, but he was being dragged deeper and deeper into the machine. It hurt more and more, blood started to spray from his veins as his body was ripped from itself. The most painful part was when he lost part of his face and when he felt the blade sink into his intestines. Dragging them partly out of his belly. Toby stopped screaming when his throat was torn out and his lungs filled with his blood.

Freddie didn't let go of him for a couple of minutes. Gwenda had noticed the combine had stopped and she came out to check what had happened. When she saw the two of them...god.

The depression sank in a day after Toby had died.

Freddie had found help by drinking, whisky had become his best friend and so had reading. He would keep himself busy in the day by doing the farm work and driving into Orington with Thomas, Victor and Richard Brent.

But when night came, he decided he would sit in the living room. A book in one hand a bottle of whisky in the other, no glass required. He didn't read for more than an hour, once the hour had passed he would drink from the bottle. The whisky went down well, warm and smooth on the tongue.

Toby took a hold of the bark with his good arm and spoke once more, his voice remained the same only a little dry but he shouted this time.

"BARN! BARN! BARN! BARN! BARN!"

His mouth dropped open and he was now screaming the words that bounced around Freddie's head like a bad pain. Freddie held his head and screamed.

He turned around and began to run he was running through the forest and the snow was starting to fall swiftly. The cold air whipped his skin and it stung his flesh. Freezing temperatures, it was dropping fast. Freddie somehow found the strength to run towards his land.

He would take the more direct route, the same way he came but take a shortcut by heading towards the lake then back around to the stairs. The stairs would take him to the barn. What was in the barn?

Freddie reached the stairs within sixty seconds, he wasn't as far away as he had first thought.

When running up the stairs he had almost slipped a few times but managed to regain his balance by grabbing the metal pole he had placed for support. Once he reached the top he could see the barn, the cabin for the Brent brothers and the farmhouse. He ran towards the barn but slipped on the snow, he landed on his face and felt as the coldness hit him. The blizzard was starting to get worse now. The snow was falling heavily and the winter winds were starting to pick up. Once he reached the side of the barn he pushed his body against the side entrance door. Inside there was a deathly silence and a faint metallic rotten smell in the air. The smell reminded him of the day Toby had died in his arms...

No, stop thinking about that. It wasn't your fault, thought Freddie.

He started to walk along the base of the barn, looking around for anything. There must be something here. Then he saw something, crumpled up at the base of the stairs that lead to the platform that was the second floor of the barn. It looked like some clothing, wait, a hand. Is that...

When he looked closer at the pile at the base of the stairs, he gasped with horror. Hugo Brent lay there. His body was leaning against the wall. His head was missing. Blood had covered the majority of his torso and the wall and floor around him. Freddie held his mouth then vomited. Richard was close by, lying across the floorboards. His stomach was slashed open, his insides spilling all over the floorboards. Blood dripping on the floor below. He couldn't see what he looked like exactly. He could just see him through the small gaps in the floorboards, but after seeing Hugo. That was more than enough. Freddie ran to the barn doors, he forced one open and saw two figures standing near the house.

One was Edna, he could make that out. But the other was tall and bulky, Thomas?

Freddie opened his mouth and shouted, "DEAD!"

14

Francis Rogers had a weird dream last night.

He was on the Martin farm, he had never seen that place before in his life but now it was almost as if it was part of him. He had of course spoken to Edna and even performed various sexual acts with the girl. But this was in his own home, no one in the entire of Orington knew what the two were up too.

Francis knew that she loved him, or he thought that. She had said he had pushed her down some stairs and of course the entire of that stupid fucking village believed her!

He continued to ride his motorbike through the snow, it was getting heavy now, almost turning into a blizzard. He had to wipe it from his visor on his helmet every now and then. Francis had been dreaming of the farm for a good seven days now, but it was only last night when the dreams took a turn for the worst.

In the dream he was walking across the fields, his hands running over the wheat as he took soft graceful steps.

It took him a few moments to realise he was completely naked, but in the dream, it seemed normal. His nude body strolled through the fields, the sun was warm and soothing on his soft skin. Everything was normal and everything was beautiful.

Until he closed his eyes.

When his eyelids opened the world around him transformed, the wheat died and the sun turned into the moon. Inky blackness infected the sky and he suddenly felt cold. He found he was slowly changing, his toes folded under his feet and his fingers bent in unnatural positions. Bending and twisting into different directions. His back bent and his spin pushed against the flesh, he folded inwards and landed on the cold earth.

He tried to speak but his tongue had twisted into his mouth and pushed itself onto the roof.

"Oh...g...dd....wat...is...ppenning..."

His words bubbled in his mouth as he tried to work out what was happening, the dream seemed to only get worse as he tried to stand. His body weak and bones shattered in his knees and elbows. He collapsed onto the floor and begged for help. The thought of death was near.

When he finally woke up he was in a sweat, his skin was sweating and his light grey t-shirt had turned dark on the collar, armpits and back. He ran his hands over his face and went into the bathroom, turned on the cold tap and ran cold water over his burning skin. Francis felt as if he was coming down with the flu, but he didn't feel ill.

That was when he decided to go and see Edna Martin. He had to speak to her, no matter what her parents said to him. If he didn't speak to her and clear this matter up, his name would be blacklisted all over Orington until he left or died. And at this moment in time, this was not an option. He wasn't in a finical situation to even consider leaving the village, this accusation had torn his life apart. His family believed him of course but the constant egg throwing at the windows and the odd watermelon at the house was enough to make them enraged with him. Not because they stopped believing him. But because of what he had gotten himself into, a young girl who was pretty. His mother had told him he was a stupid man who was only thinking about sex. That was not the case, he knew he loved her. At the time at least.

The worst-case he had was when he was called by some boys in the park (he had never told his parents or brother about this. He was ashamed to admit). The boys were all around 16-19 years old and there was five of them. The first boy with the pimple-covered face said, "You're the baby killer aren't you?"

"No, she slipped and fell. It was an accident!" replied Francis.

"Do you like pushing women carrying babies downstairs Rogers?" said the short fat one as he stood up from his bike.

"It was an accident. How many times do you need to be told? She slipped. She tumbled down the stairs."

The largest boy stood up, his hands were bulky and matched his body tone. He wasn't fat, or muscular. He just seemed naturally large.

"Did you rape her?" he said as he gritted his teeth.

"What? No, I'm not like that!"

"Well, we wouldn't put it past you Rogers. We know what your kind is like. Acting all innocent then you go and do it again. You could do it to Mike's single mum here. Or get my older sister!"

Francis was sick and tired, he turned on his heels and began to walk out of the park. Going here was a bad idea, but he thought going here might help him think about his relationship with Edna and where it began to sour.

"Oi hold on! We aren't finished with you yet you fucking raping baby killer!"

CRACK!

He felt something hard strike him in the back of the head when he turned around to see what it was, one of the boys was holding a small wooden baseball bat.

Francis tried to stand but one of them stomped on his face busting his nose. Blood poured out of his nostrils and covered his mouth, he scrambled on his knees and began to crawl whilst attempting to stand. His hands digging into the grassy hill as he stood on his feet. CRACK!

The bat struck him in his hip and caused severe pain to strike his entire left side. His moan for help was ignored. "Fuck this guy up!" shouted the pimple one.

The others joined in as their feet, fists and the wooden bat struck his body. His face was bloody and bruised, battered and swollen. Francis' body lay across the grass limp and sore, his stomach ached and his face had gone completely numb. That was when he heard something, although his vision was a blur and his hearing was fuzzy he could still hear something. It was a zipper on someone's jeans. He heard it but it was faint then a voice came. He couldn't put the voice to one of their faces, "I'm...fuck...mouth."

The sentence was broken, yet the words he heard was enough to make him realise what was going to happen next. He began to brace himself, although he squirmed and began to turn away he felt some of them hold him in place. Then he felt something slip into his mouth, it tasted awful. It was sweaty, that was just the smell. The taste was worse. The thing in his mouth was limp at first, like a thick noodle. Then it began to get harder as it moved back and forth in his mouth. Sliding over his tongue-

"Shit," he said as he came to the gate to the Martin farm.

He entered the land by opening the gate himself then riding his bike along the road that was now covered in a thick layer of white. The virgin snow was destroyed under the tires on his bike, he felt it slip now and again but he managed to gain control. When he stopped outside of the farm he heard the front door open and an all too familiar voice say, "Francis?"

Francis got off of his bike after turning the engine off. He removed his helmet.

15

Edna Martin was standing on the porch looking at someone she had not seen for a long time. She intended on keeping it that way. But now he was here, in the flesh. He was standing wearing his light blue jeans (they had turned white on the knees), his boots were dirty and stained with oil. He rolled up his sleeves on his baggy jacket to expose those thick hairy arms, a silver watch on his left wrist and leather bands on his right. He was still handsome and just as big, he had put a little weight on but that didn't affect his looks that much. His cheeks had gone a little chubby and his face had stubble from not shaving for a few days. Edna walked down the steps and stopped around two meters in front of him.

He placed his helmet on the handlebar on his bike and said, "We need to talk." His voice still had that soft tone to it.

"Now is not the time Francis. I'm not just saying that to make you go home. I'm serious. We have a lot going on right now."

"But...I really want to talk to you...you don't understand the severity of your actions. You're still a girl."

"Francis! Please!"

"What's going on?" he asked as he took two steps towards her.

Edna sighed and ran her hand over her face, "It's Agatha. She's gone missing. She's not in the house. Or the barn. My dad has gone looking for her in the forest behind our house."

"Oh god! Let me help," he reached out towards her but she pulled away.

"That's not all Francis. Heather has been involved in an accident. She's hurt herself. She's been knocked unconscious. We can't get in contact with the doctors in Orington. Go! Just go!"

"I can help you! I can take her into the village!"

"No! You'll...you'll hurt her!"

Francis was taken back by those words.

"You don't honestly believe I would do such a thing do you?"

Edna shrugged her shoulders and said, "You tried to kill me. To get rid of the baby. You killed our child!"

"That's not fair!" he screamed.

"Life isn't fucking fair Francis! You hurt me! You broke me!"

"What do you think you did to me? I was attacked every day when word got out! Francis Rogers the baby killer!"

"You deserved it!"

"Edna. Do you have any idea what else they did to me? DO YOU!"

Edna seemed to feel empathy for a second, her eyes went wide and her mouth cracked open. But she managed to pull herself back, "No. And I don't care!"

"I was orally raped by a group of teenagers. They beat me up with a bat, they kicked me. They punched me. Then one of them forced his fucking cock in my mouth until he..." he stopped himself. He felt himself getting worked up, the lump in his throat and the beating in his chest as it seemed to get tight.

"They...what?"

"They beat me. They raped me. I couldn't fight back. I want to make things right. You need to tell the truth," he was taking steps closer to her now.

"I told the truth. I told them that you pushed me. Because you did," her teeth sank into her bottom lip.

The blizzard was getting worse now, the two of them had to use their arms to shield their faces.

Then they heard someone shout, "DEAD! THEY ARE DEAD!"

The two of them looked at one another then towards the barn, a figure was running towards them. He had his arms wrapped around his body and his teeth were chattering.

Edna looked at her dad and said, "Who's dead!"

"Richard and Hugo! And..."

He didn't need to continue for Edna to know who else was dead. It was more than clear that her little sister was now gone.

"Tell me it's not true..." her words faded from her mouth.

"I'm sorry Edna," Francis touched her shoulder and pulled her towards him.

She screamed and pushed him away, "Get away from me! You fucking animal!"

Freddie looked towards Francis and he knew who the man was. Freddie grabbed Francis by the shoulders then punched him in the face, "You tried to kill my daughter!" the punch was weak but he still felt it as the knuckles collided with his cheek.

"NO!" shouted Francis, "Tell him the truth, Edna. Tell him the truth!"

"I was told the truth," said Freddie as he grabbed Francis by the collar.

"All of it?" questioned Francis.

Freddie's grip loosened and he said, "What really happened?"

The front door opened and Gwenda came out she was crying and said, "Did you find Agatha?"

Freddie walked up the steps and held his wife by the waist and said, "I did."

She didn't need to be told any more. She could see it in his eyes. Then she broke down in a fit of uncontrollable sobbing.

16

Thomas Martin had a feeling of being unwell.

He thought it could be the flu, but he had been vomiting for the past hour and his skin had gone sickly white. He had severe diarrhoea that later turned into a fluid. He had even snapped at Michelle a few times, he knew she was only doing her best. By helping him into the bathroom when he wanted to vomit, he held him and she would use a cold cloth to dab him down. His skin was burning up and his blood felt as if it had turned into boiling water. Michelle dabbed his forehead with the cloth and ran it over his cheeks and neck before she placed it back into the bucket. She shivered.

"You can close the window darling," he said as he licked his dry lips. They were starting to peel and crack now.

"But you're burning up," she held her hand on his forehead and continued, "You're sweating and hot Tom. I don't think this is the flu. It seems worse."

"What do you think it could be?" he said as his teeth chattered away.

"I'm...I don't know..."

What was happening to Thomas Martin seemed almost impossible to Michelle. He was shivering due to the coldness coming from the window but his skin was sweating from the virus that was in his body. She closed the window with a heavy bang and said, "There's a blizzard starting up outside."

"No chance of getting into Orington now then. The truck won't be getting through it," said Thomas. He lifted his head and coughed loudly. When he looked at his hand, there was a patch of blood on his palm and his fingers.

"Here, drink this," said Michelle as she handed him a glass of water. He took it from her and took a mouthful but spat it back out almost straight away.

"I'm getting worried. You can't keep anything down. I'm surprised you are still vomiting," said Michelle as she wiped the water from the floor.

"I'm in so much pain, Michelle. I feel like my insides are on fire. There must be something I can take."

"You took painkillers and you threw them back up. It's almost as if your body is rejecting things you put into it."

"I'm scared..." his voice was almost a whisper now. He closed his eyes and tears started to well up.

"It's okay. Once the blizzard clears we can get you a doctor," she leaned forward to kiss him but he turned his head away.

"Sorry...I don't want you getting it...I'm aching all over...I can't feel my hands and feet..."

His hands were trembling and his feet were too.

"It's okay I understand," she pulled herself away and fixed her dress by pulling it back down to her knees.

The two of them had not heard of the news regarding the

deaths of Richard and Hugo Brent and Agatha.
"Did you dream last night?" asked Thomas.
Michelle sighed, "I did."
"What did you dream of?"
"I dreamt of pain. Suffering and the inner demons that peel us apart from the insides."
There was a sudden feeling of tension, she had said those words firmly and it startled Thomas. He even sat himself up in his bed and looked at her as she looked at the heavy snowfall outside. Watching as the ground started to turn white with the unbroken snow.
She didn't need to explain to him, and he didn't want an explanation from her. Because deep down he had an idea of what she meant, and that idea scared him.
"Michelle. I'm going..." he held his hand to his throat.
Michelle turned and quickly helped him into the bathroom. The trip wasn't that far. Just three doors down, but with Thomas almost limping it seemed to take a lot longer. She supported him by holding his waist and he had his hand over her shoulder. His hair was plastered to his face and he had to brush it out of his eyes now and again.
Michelle opened the door and they were met with a cool winters breeze as it whipped through the open window. The same window that Agatha Martin was dragged out of hours before. Thomas placed his head into the toilet and began to vomit.
Michelle knelt beside him and ran her fingers through his hair with one hand and held his hand with the other. Their fingers inter winded.
She loved him.
And he loved her.
She wouldn't change him for the world, he had his

imperfections but who didn't? He was a human being at the end of the day, and a good one.

She could remember everything they did together, from sitting in the park to sitting in the barn and making love for the first time. They were good times and she wouldn't want them to ever disappear. But she had her favourite memory with Thomas.

And that was when he met her parents for the first time. She had invited him to meet her family in a type of traditional way. Through having dinner at the Shallicker family home. Marge and Patrick Shallicker were very well known people, he had met Patrick a few times and even spoken to him. But he was now seeing her daughter.

Michelle thought it might be a little awkward for the pair of them. Thomas sat next to Michelle at the six-seater dinner table and they all spoke freely. But Thomas continued to say please and thank you with formality. Patrick said, "There is no need for that formal shit Tom. I know who your mum and dad are. And trust me, lad. They have mouths as dirty as your pigs,"

From that day on Thomas spoke to Patrick and Marge in the same way he spoke to Michelle.

Thomas continued to gag and cry out as his stomach became tighter and tighter. The vomit had turned into bile and burnt as it came out of his mouth.

Michelle held his body and he tensed up, his muscles stood as hard as stone. He gestured for her to give him some space, she rose and turned on the cold tap. Ready to dab his skin. But as she twisted the top, no water came out and the metal felt cold to touch. She tried the hot water and she had the same results.

Then she noticed the window, the glass was starting to

become frosted and it was growing like fungus across the pane. She could suddenly see her breath in front of her and she started to panic. Her skin turned dry and her hairs became erect. Trying desperately to catch as many heat particles as possible.

"Thomas...I..." her words became dead in her mouth. He had stopped moving, his body was limp and he lay on his stomach across the bathroom floor.

"Thomas. OH GOD!" she ran across to him and knelt by his body. She started to shake him and he moaned loudly. His mouth opened wide, wider than Michelle thought was humanly possible. He looked over to her, his eyes rolled to the side and he groaned. Like a dying animal, then he folded in half. His head was touching his feet and Michelle pulled herself backwards, her feet scrambled across the floor and she used her elbows as support. He began to change, his body began to violently change and morph. When he looked up at her, his eyes were almost bleeding. They were bloodshot. He reached out and gargled at her, Michelle could only scream, "OH MY GOD!"

She crawled out of the room and began to run towards the stairs, tears streamed down her face and she had knocked her glasses off at some point. But she didn't care. She heard the thumping and cries of Thomas as he struggled in the bathroom.

Once she reached the top of the stairs she felt something wrap around her mouth and something hard jam into her back. It took her around three seconds to realise it was the barrel of a gun. She pulled herself free and heard someone scream. Not cry out. Not say. Or screech. But scream her name "MICHELLE!" and it terrified her. She spun around and kicked it in the stomach as hard as she could.

What she saw was something that came from her nightmare. Thomas Martin stood before her, his body twisted. His mouth gaping wide and his eyes bloodshot as he panted and moaned. In his hands, he held the hunting crossbow and he pointed it towards her, the bolt was aimed at her heart.

Michelle's eyes went wide. Thomas' facial expression never changed, he pointed the crossbow to his parent's room and said "Now. Or I will kill you!" his voice never changed. It was the same delightful tone it had been last night and the thousand times before. That was why she was scared, his body and eyes suggested pain but his voice said otherwise.

As soon as the two of them was in his parent's bedroom, only one of the rifles remained on the rack. Thomas had a tight grip of the other, Michelle also noticed a cut-throat razor sticking out of his pocket.

He aimed his gun at the armchair and she sat herself on it, she felt a great deal of fear flood her body and she said, "Thomas. Please..."

"Shut up...GOD, IT BURNS...RUN!...MICHELLE!...if you move I will...OH GOD...PLEASE...STOP...I'M SORRY...PLEASE FORGIVE ME...kill you..."

His words was a cruel mixture of pain and a hint of normality. His behaviour was getting increasingly scary, Michelle didn't know how to react to the situation. Thomas turned away and even through his t-shirt she could see something moving under his skin. Not like small mites, no. It was two hands forcing their way around his body, then she saw it take hold of his neck. Her eyes went wide, she had to cover her mouth with her hands to keep herself quiet. The hand seemed to take a tight grip and Thomas cried out in pain once more. "NO...MICHELLE RUN...NOW!" She knew that was the real Thomas and she believed him. She jumped from the armchair and ran across the bedroom, the door was ajar and she reached out to pull it open.

FFFTTT!

Something stiff and powerful struck her calf, she slammed into the door and as a result, she closed it. Her leg hurt and when she checked, there was a crossbow bolt sticking out of her calf. Blood pouring from the wound and changing her light green dress a dark red, Thomas stood over her and he said, "Next time. I will kill you...MICHELLE!"

17

"Where was she?" asked Gwenda Martin as she sat down next to Heather, she ran her fingers through her daughter's hair.

"She was...she was pinned on a tree...her body...was..." For the conversation to be held, Freddie had asked Edna, Francis and Victor to go into the kitchen and wait.

"Oh god...I can't...I just..." Gwenda began to shake. Freddie sat next to her and wrapped his arms around her trembling body, it was almost as if he was holding an injured bird. Trying to make sure it was okay.

"I know...I know..."

"What's happening to us, Freddie? Three people are dead! One of them our daughter!"

"I don't know Gwen. I really don't know," Freddie held back the fear in his tone. He had no choice. Because he was scared of what he had witnessed today was enough to bring anyone to their knees in fear. To Freddie, this

wasn't the work of a man or an animal. It would explain
the dreams, Agatha's disappearance and even the brutal
deaths of Hugo and Richard. Along with the
hallucinations of Toby he had been seeing. He hadn't
mentioned what he had seen in the forest besides
Agatha. Seeing her small body mangled in the tree
branches as if she had been dragged through the trees.
She must have been scared. She must have been so
scared. Her final moments were still trapped in his own
mind. He just wished his daughter had died a quick and
painless death, but seeing that. He highly doubted that
Agatha had died a quick and painless death. He couldn't
get her face out of his head. Pale face, sunken eyes and
blue lips. He should have taken her down and brought
her back, but when he passed out he was almost like he
was dragged into another world. Taken from the reality
of the forest and forced into a world that has no limits.
"What if there's someone on the farm? They are going to
kill us!" cried Gwenda.
"Gwenda! Pull yourself together! We need to get off the
farm, now! I'll work with Francis and Victor to get the
truck started. Edna can go and fetch Thomas and
Michelle. No one else needs to die," said Freddie as he
held his wife tightly to his chest, "Stay here. Keep an
eye on Heather. If things seem to get worse make sure
you let me know. Okay?"
"What will we do if we can't get the truck started?"
asked Gwenda as she rubbed the tears from her eyes.
"We'll cross that bridge when we come to it. At the
moment our survival is the most important thing. We
need to get out of here. Something's hunting us," as soon
as he said those last three words he immediately
regretted it. He held his mouth shut and turned his head

away. He felt Gwenda's breath on the side of his neck, "What?"

Freddie sighed and held his hand over his mouth, "I said something is hunting us."

"Something?"

"It's not an animal. I've seen what it can do."

"Not a man? Or an animal? Then what is it?"

"Gwenda, I have no idea what it is. But it can kill without mercy. Agatha was dragged 30ft into the trees, her body was...shit! Richard was torn almost in half and Hugo's head was cut off!"

"Oh no...oh no...I can't..." she rested her head in her hands and began to sob.

"I'll get the others. We can work on the truck..." he held her head and knelt down so their eyes met.

"Gwenda. You need to keep yourself together. I'm just as scared as you are. Be strong. For me. For Heather. For Tom, Edna and Vic. Okay?"

She nodded in his hands and kissed his thumb. That was all he needed for reassurances.

Gwenda reached across to Heather and held her hand on her forehead, the girl was panting heavily her skin was soaked in sweat and she felt hot.

"Freddie, she's got a fever."

Freddie was about to speak when he suddenly felt a strong cold breeze as if someone had opened the door. The breeze blew around the living room and the fire blew out as quickly as someone blowing out a candle. The windows began to frost over from the inside and their breaths clouded in front of their faces. The temperature began to drop rapidly and they felt their skin getting cold. The two of them looked at each other. Shivering together, yet Heather's skin was burning up.

"I'm going to speak with them. Stay here. Keep an eye on Heather."

Freddie slipped out of the living room and headed up the hall towards the kitchen. Gwenda could still hear him. Gwenda kept one hand on Heather and the other hand gripped on the arm of the couch.

Why did this have to happen?

Gwenda looked at the three dogs, all of them curled up and asleep, they had not reacted to the temperature drop in any way. Gwenda reached out with her foot and tapped Stella on her back with her toes, the dog lifted her head and looked up at Gwenda. But there was no reaction. Just those large brown eyes looking at her. Stella pressed her head back down. The dog seemed to be in pain, or even ill. It was affecting the dogs too. Gwenda looked at Sam and Lucy. The two of them were curled up around the dead fire, the smell of ember was thick in the air. She looked at Heather, she was like a heat source, she was burning up. Hair sticking to sweaty skin, Gwenda checked her daughter's head. The blood was drying up on the bandage and she decided to change it. Once she removed it she felt the skull.

The fracture was serious and would possibly require surgery to fix. A metal plate would be needed.

Although Gwenda didn't want her daughter to die or forget anything. She did pray for her to forget two things and those were how she ended up in this situation, and the second was the abuse Gwenda had performed on Heather in the past two years.

Heather was a fussy child when growing up, always crying for food or sleep. One day things got a little out of control. The baby cried in her high chair, Gwenda grabbed Heather by the waist and shook her violently.

Her head snapped forth and back and she screamed. Gwenda screamed "Shut the fuck up!" before throwing the infant across the floor as if she was a bowling ball. Heather slammed into the drawers.

Her mother walked over to her, her head aching and tears streaming down her cheeks from the amount of stress she had been put through that morning. Heather continued to cry, from the pain that been inflicted onto her. Heather was crumpled up, her bones were still developing and could break easily. Gwenda didn't think of that at the time and instead tried to force-feed the girl with a jar of baby food, forcing spoonful after spoonful into the girl's mouth. Her face was caked orange from the mush inside the jar. Heather continued to cry only it was more muffled.

From that day on, Gwenda changed her mindset on Heather. The child was difficult and hard to handle. It was why she snapped so easily. Plus the death of Toby had forever remained with her. Guilt played a big part in Heather's last two years upbringing. Gwenda was filled with it, from throwing her youngest child onto the floor and forcing mushed up baby food into her mouth.

She tried to put it past her but she feared it would soon catch up with her. No one but herself and Heather knew of this, but Heather had never spoken of it. She was only four years old after all. But things like that would stick with her, raising a child was not easy. Yet, maybe because Gwenda had it easy with the previous four children. They had all been good babies, sleeping all night and eating when it was feeding time. Yes, they had their days where they would not eat or not sleep and would cry instead. But that was rarely the case with any of them. She couldn't understand why Heather was so different on so many levels.

The truth only struck a few weeks after the incident, and it made Gwenda close to having a heart attack. She noticed the differences in the girl, she was similar to both Edna and Agatha. But not too much. She hardly resembled Thomas and Victor, Gwenda just brushed that aside to their genders. Then it clicked.

She couldn't figure out why she didn't notice beforehand. And if she knew whilst she was pregnant she would have terminated the pregnancy right away. Heather's biological father was Hugo Brent.

18

When Freddie Martin entered the kitchen, the three of them were sat on the counter. Edna was next to Victor and Francis was next to Victor. They were not speaking to one another and seemed to have been sitting in silence through the full duration of his conversation with Gwenda.

"Me and your mum, Gwenda, have an idea," said Freddie as he stood in the doorway.

"What is it?" asked Victor as he jumped from the countertop.

"We are going to try and get the truck started."

"What, with the blizzard?" asked Edna.

"We have no other choice sweetheart. I'm going to need your help, Francis. I know we may not see eye to eye for what you did to Edna. But we need to stick together. You aren't my priority either. But we can help each other out. Do you understand?" Freddie's voice was strong and firm.

"I do sir," Francis said as he rubbed his face from being punched earlier.

110

"Good, now I'm going to need you all to take part in this. Victor and Francis you two come with me. Edna, you go and get Thomas and Michelle. Do you all understand? I'll get my tools from the cellar. Vic and Francis go outside, here are the keys for the truck," he handed them to Victor.

The four of them went to do their thing. Francis left through the front door with Victor right behind him. The wind howled outside and the cold was even greater than it was before. Their skin turned cold and numb instantly. Victor slammed the door shut.

Edna headed upstairs and Freddie slid the bolt to the side (it was placed there to avoid Heather from opening the door when she worked out how handles worked) and opened the door. It was dark in the cellar and seemed to have an even colder temperature. Freddie shivered, even more, his teeth clattering and his arms hugged his body. The cellar was a small thing and used only for storage, they had their Christmas decorations down there and some wooden boxes filled with old clothing. He began his descent into the cellar, the wooden steps creaked after each step he took.

He first came to an open box, he peered inside and removed the sheet that covered the top. Inside there were three torches, he guessed they would need them. He picked them up and placed them under his arm before looking for the toolbox. Once he found it he quickly headed back upstairs.

"Dad!" screamed Edna.

Freddie threw the items on the floor and ran to the stairs. There was a strange sense of deja vu from the dream he had earlier today. Once he got onto the second floor, Edna had hidden herself in her bedroom. He saw her

show her head and she said, "Dad! Help!"
"What's happening?"
"It's Thomas...he's got a crossbow!"
He saw a bolt sticking out of the floor near Edna's door.
Where he had attempted to shoot her, "Shit. Have you
been shot?"
"No, but Michelle...she's hurt...I don't know what's
wrong with him," Edna kept herself in the bedroom.
"Okay, come here. I'll get Michelle," Freddie
outstretched his arms for her.
Edna took one step in the hallway and turned her head
slightly to see if she could see Thomas. He wasn't in
sight, she made a run for it and as she reached the stairs
she felt a sharp pain in her shoulder. The tip tore through
the skin and she could see it coming out of her shoulder.
Her t-shirt flooded with bright red blood where the tip
had penetrated her skin. She felt the wetness spread.
The bolt looked more like an antenna coming out of her
back rather than something fired from a crossbow.
"Edna!" cried Freddie. He quickly grabbed her by the
arm and pulled her forward, he cradled her body and
placed her behind him.
"Are you okay?" she nodded as she held the arrow,
"Don't pull it out. Not yet anyway. Stay here. If he
comes out just make a run for it. Okay?" she nodded.
Freddie hugged her and slowly walked across the
hallway, from the floor he pulled out the bolt and held it
like a knife. The door to his bedroom was slightly open
and he heard Michelle's cries inside. Freddie took a deep
breath and entered the bedroom slowly. He saw
Michelle, she was tied to the armchair in the far corner
of his bedroom. Her hands tied to the arms and her
ankles tied to the wooden legs at the bottom. Her leg

was covered in blood at the calf. Right, where a crossbow bolt had been shot. She also had one in her shoulder and another in her arm. Her glasses had been knocked off and her face was red and sweating.

He needed to help her. And fast. As he opened the door more, he could see Thomas. He was standing near the mirror. What Freddie saw was not his son. Thomas Martin was twisted, his body looked like it was causing him a great deal of pain. Thomas used the crossbow to smash the mirror, and when it shattered shards of it covered the floor. Small sections of reflection covered the flooring and some skidded under the bed.

Freddie slowly entered his bedroom he looked at his bed, there was a small set of drawers on his side of the bed. He opened the top drawer removed the revolver. It was a Smith & Wesson M19 .357 Magnum to be exact. He slipped it into his jeans pocket and walked over to Michelle. When he got to her he covered her mouth with his hand and gestured for her to be quiet. Her eyes were wide.

He used the tip of the bolt to free her. She had only been tied down with tape. But there was a lot of it. Once he got the layers off, the two of them headed towards the door. Their hearts in their mouths and their hands had turned clammy. The fear of being seen was there.

He didn't seem to notice as they slipped out of the door and headed into the hallway, Edna was still at the top of the stairs. Staring at them. Her skin was sickly white and she looked terrified, "Behind you!" she suddenly shouted.

Freddie grabbed Michelle by the hand and the two of them ran down the hallway, Michelle was crying in pain from the bolts that had penetrated her body. Freddie heard the crossbow go off again.

Michelle let out a cry as she struck the floor and rolled onto her side before slamming into the wall. Freddie stopped and turned, but he felt a strange sensation. As if he was floating. His body levitated into the air and he flew across the hall. His body struck the bannister and he landed on the stairs behind Edna. Michelle screamed as her body was dragged back into the bedroom. Each of the bolts digging deeper and deeper into her skin. She felt the pain, fearing that one of them would snap off and she wouldn't be able to pull them out. The door slammed shut behind her.

Freddie lay on his back and cried out in pain. He lifted himself up and looked at Edna, she was holding her hands over her face and was crying. The two of them held one another and cried together, Edna sniffled, "He's gone! It's taken him!"

Freddie held his daughter's head into his chest and said, "I know darling. I know. Come on. We can't stay here. We need to get out of here. Get the truck started and go."

"What about Michelle?"

"I...I...maybe..."

"I know," she said suddenly as if she understood what was to come of Michelle Shallicker. There was no saving her, that was clear. Most of the guns had been placed in his bedroom. The revolver was in his pocket from earlier, he forgot he had taken it with him. But there was no point in using it. Thomas was no longer human, he had qualities that could only be described as a monster. A monster with evil abilities.

There was no point in trying to save Michelle now. The girl was going to die.

The father and daughter headed downstairs and into the

living room. Gwenda was now holding Heather on her lap and when she saw the two of them she said, "What's going on?"

"It's Thomas. It's got him. He shot us with a crossbow!" Gwenda could only cry, she lifted Heather and buried her face in the blankets that her daughter was wrapped in, "I'll go and see what I can find in the medical tin," said Freddie as he headed into the dining room and then entered the kitchen. As he opened the cupboard door, he heard the front door open and Victor soon appeared in the doorway, "Oh..."

"I'm okay. Stay away from Thomas," said Freddie firmly.

"What's wrong with him?" asked Victor as he came closer.

"I don't know. He's gone mad. He's not human. Whatever is happening on this farm Victor. It's not going to stop. Not until we are all dead. Stay away from him!" Victor could only nod as Freddie looked through the cupboard for the medical tin, when he found it he flipped the lid open.

"The toolbox is near the cellar. Take it and see what you can do."

"That's the thing, dad. The car. I don't think we will be able to fix it. Not tonight anyway," he said as he sighed.

"Why not?"

"The engine has become frozen solid, the petrol has frozen and the doors are sealed shut. We even tried the doors to the Brent's car. But that's in the same condition."

"Shit. Okay, wait in the living room. I need to help Edna."

Victor didn't reply. He left the doorway.

Freddie was looking through the medical tin, there was a small metal container and when he opened it there was a syringe inside. The container was used for cleaning the needle so it could be re-used. There were also two small glass bottles next to it, both of them read: MORPHINE. From the side cupboard, he took out a bottle of vodka and doubled checked for bandages, most of them had been used on Heather. But there should be enough.

He closed the tin and took it with him into the living room, the survivors were all gathered around the coffee table. Their faces told everything.

Freddie approached Edna, he placed the tin down on the table and opened it up, "This might...never mind that...this is going to hurt. Okay?"

She nodded and turned her head away, Freddie pulled it out as quickly as possible and quickly washed it with vodka, whilst Victor held Edna's hand. Francis was seated on the floor by the window and staring blankly at the situation unfolding before him.

Freddie poured some Vodka onto a cloth and washed out in the wound quickly before wrapping a bandage around it. It was the most he could do for now.

"Okay, that was good of you. It's the least I could do. If it gets painful or hot let me know. Here, take two of these," between his fingers was some white plastic. With capsules inside of it and sealed inside by some foil.

She popped two out and slipped them into her mouth, she swallowed them dryly.

The next turn of events was enough to drive terror into each of them, as the back door opened and they heard a loud moaning. The dog's ears pricked up and they snarled, and a dark shadow moved past the window quickly. They all looked at one another with wide eyes

and pumping hearts.
They could hear feet dragging down the hall and
something banging on the front door whilst making a
horrible crying-choking sound. The moans from the
kitchen only got tenser. Gwenda rose and held Heather
to her chest tightly, Freddie picked up the fire poker
from the mantle and handed it to Victor.
From his pocket, Freddie removed the revolver, he
snapped open the chamber and counted just six bullets.
Oh god...

19

It was the dogs that attacked first.
Lucy jumped upwards at Victor, but with one quick
swing of the fire poker, he shattered the dog's skull.
It lay crumpled in the corner of the room and when it
lifted it's head its eyes were black. Its lips peeled
backwards exposing rows of sharp and jagged teeth.
Francis grabbed the marble clock from the chest of
drawers pushed up against the wall and with two brutal
strikes, he crushed the dog's head into a bloody pulp.
Stella and Sam then attacked, one grabbed Francis by
the wrist and the other jumped up at his leg. Teeth tore
through flesh and his clothing. He let out a horrifying
scream as blood sprayed from his wounds and onto the
floor. Victor beat Sam over the back and he let go.
Turning his attention towards Victor, the dog howled
and Stella tore off Francis' thumb and part of his palm.
Before the two of them began to walk towards Victor,
who was backing up into the corner. Freddie was about
to fire his revolver when a set of wet hands grabbed his
shoulder. When he turned he let out a scream.
Edna and Gwenda reacted in the same way.

Francis pulled himself up against the wall, holding his torn arm and leg with his good hand. His eyes were filled with tears and blood pumped out of his wound. The thing that grabbed Freddie was the Brent brothers. They were both naked, they were fused to one another by their backs and elbows and was walking like a crab. Their skin had turned pale and their hands had grown claws. Freddie fired once, the bullet struck the Richard and Hugo- thing in the hip but it didn't react. Edna held the crossbow bolt that had been shot into her body. Stella dived into the air, Victor lifted the poker into the air and with one brutal swing, the bar struck her in her skull. This time he made sure the dog was dead, he lifted it again and hit it in her skull once more. But the dog still didn't die. Instead, it stood up on her back legs, she snarled and jumped on top of Victor. Paws on his shoulders and a jaw snapping before his face. A mixture of blood and saliva dripped onto his face as he held the dog up by the throat.

Freddie fell backwards, the brothers walking in slowly with their arms flying around and Richard was moaning as if he was in pain. Hugo's feet were being dragged across the floor as he slowly came towards them. Edna ran to the Brent brothers and forced a bolt through Richard's throat, but he only bled.

Gwenda held Heather close to her body and she pulled herself behind the couch and made sure she was out of sight. She held Heather's head to her head and began to hush the girl. Heather was beginning to wake up and the pain of the fall was about to hit her.

Victor held the dog up and pinned her on her back, his arm jammed into her throat. He pushed as hard as he could his face starting to turn red as he forced as much as his body on her. He felt for his poker, he grabbed the handle and forced the sharp end into the dog's throat and up through her mouth. She stopped moving and rolled over on her side, Victor pulled himself away and began to cry.

The Brent brothers lunged forward, clawing at Edna, their nails digging into her flesh and tearing skin away. Richard then opened his mouth up. His body was getting closer and closer to falling on top of Edna. But Edna was strong. She rammed the brothers back into the dining room and the two of them tumbled over when they hit a chair. Freddie fired once more, this time hitting them in the chest.

Four left! He thought.

He tucked the revolver in his jeans and ran into the kitchen before returning it with a large kitchen knife in one hand and a meat cleaver in the other. He handed Edna the kitchen knife and said, "Hit it! Just fucking hit it until it's dead!"

The two of them began to hit the creature, each strike was strong and powerful. The blades sliced through its flesh turning it from white to a dark red. Edna brought the knife up through Richard's throat and twisted. Blood sprayed from the wound and poured all over the floor. Leaving a bloody mess on the floor, it drenched her from he knees down. It looked like she had dipped herself into a bucket of red paint.

She tore the knife free and brought it into his eye. Richard moaned quietly, his hands then clasped around Edna's slim waist. His nails tearing into flesh, he brought his face forward and tried to bite her neck. His teeth tapped together in a way that was not humanly possible. Edna let out a cry for help.

119

Back in the living room, Victor had stayed in his position of crying whilst the dogs watched on with their teeth showing. Francis was becoming weak from the loss of blood, he tried to keep himself awake but his eyes began to open and close as his eyelids seemed to become heavier and heavier. His body then slumped to the side.

Gwenda kissed Heather on her cheek and said, "I'll be back in a second darling. Shhh!" she placed Heather down behind the couch and crawled out towards Victor. She shook him and said, "Victor! Get up! For God's sake get up!" she shook him faster now.

The boy turned to face his mum, his eyes had gone red and his skin had turned red too. Gwenda hugged him and whispered, "Shhh, it's okay. It's okay. You did what you had to do. Shhh."

Victor cried in his mum's shoulder, as his eyes rolled up he saw something that made him gasp.

Heather looked up at the dog that towered over her, it was Lucy. Sam came from behind, the two of them had their eyes staring at the baby girl. She could feel their hot breaths on her face and could.

"Mummy..." she managed to whimper.

But Lucy's jaw had already snapped around Heather's throat. Sam was next. His jaw snapped closed around Heather's shoulder, the two dogs began to pull and tug on the young girl. She couldn't scream. Her mouth had already filled with blood.

Gwenda screamed loudly, "NO! YOU FUCKING-"

She jumped up towards the dogs. She picked up the fire poker and rammed it deep into Sam's back. It had gone so deep it had, in fact, touched the floor. Sam yelped and rolled onto his side, she tugged it out and struck Lucy

over the head. Hit after hit after hit after hit after hit...
Freddie and Edna appeared in the doorway, the two of
them covered in sweat and blood. They both held blades
in their hands and were panting.
"Francis!" cried Edna as she ran over to him. She knelt
by the young man and lifted his head.
Freddie pulled the fire poker from Gwenda's fingers and
pulled her towards him. The two of them cried into each
other. It was Victor who covered Heather's body. He
kissed her head and made sure she could not be seen.
But the cream sheets that he had used quickly began to
turn red. He grabbed a cushion from the couch and
tucked it under her head. Making sure she was
comfortable...
He felt his eyes starting to tear up. He hugged both of
his parents and cried into them. Victor turned his head to
face Edna, she was holding Francis' head and then he
pulled away. Not sure what to think.

20

The entire ordeal had lasted no more than forty seconds.
But it felt like a lifetime. They had lost one.
Beautiful baby Heather.
She lay on the couch, Freddie had placed her there. The
dogs had been dragged into the kitchen and they had
also dragged that fleshy mass of the Brent brothers in
with them. Francis had continued to slip in and out of a
conscious state.
"What do we do?" asked Edna as she held a trembling
Francis, they all looked at one another. Unsure of what
to do.
"It's clear. It's hunting us down. One by one. Four of us
are dead. One of us is insane and another is close to

death," said Freddie, he continued, "We can try once more with the truck."

"Dad, the engine has frozen. We couldn't even touch it," said Victor.

"It's true Mr Martin. You'll get an ice burn or something. Maybe we could make a run for it to the gate?" said Francis

"No, the blizzard is too much. We could easily get lost from one another and well...the outcome is what happened to everyone else who isn't alive in this room." Everyone just stood looking at one another, not knowing what to say or do. It was clear that the escape by the cars was out of the question. There was no doubt in their minds about that, then Gwenda said tearfully, "We could use ropes, tie them to our bodies and each other. Then walk to the gate."

She looked back down at Heather's covered corpse. The sheets were now almost red.

Freddie nodded in agreement and ran into the cellar, he came back up shortly after with some rope, "I also got some torches but there's only four. I'll have one. Gwenda you will have one. Francis, you'll have one too. And Edna, you can stay with Francis as he's injured. Vic, here," Freddie handed them their torches and Victor slipped his in his pocket for now. They all started to tie the rope around themselves mostly their waists or through their jeans as if it was a belt. They were more than aware that what they were going to do was more than dangerous. But they didn't have a choice, waiting it out was not an option. Freddie checked the revolver, just four bullets remained in the barrel. He didn't wish to use it. He slipped the revolver in the strap of his jeans and took hold of the meat cleaver that he used to kill the

Brent brothers. Edna had a kitchen knife, Gwenda took the fire poker and Victor had a mallet. The group headed to the front door, Freddie was at the front with Gwenda behind him and Victor was behind his mum.
Freddie grabbed the handle and pulled the door open, the wind howled and the snow was coming down heavy. The snow was knee height at least now and there was no visibility. They walked across the porch, feeling the ice and snow crunch and crack underneath their boots and trainers.
They didn't hesitate any more.
The group headed outside, closing the door behind them. Walking through the snow was a challenge. Feeling it as it soaked into their bare legs and thin fabric trousers. Their bodies began to shake and their teeth started to chatter. They didn't exchange words, it was too cold to do so. The walk across the front garden was a tough one, Victor and Francis had fallen over a few times. It was slowing them down, and the blizzard was only starting to pick up.
By now, the group could barely see one another, save for the odd beam of light cutting through the mist like air that was surrounding them. Victor looked forward, his flashlight was exposing a small amount of area around him. He could make out his mum but not his dad, he kept one hand on the torch and the other on the mallet. His fingers had become numb and he couldn't help but squeeze the handle of the mallet. He needed to get warm. The house might not have been warm, but it was warmer in there than it was out here!
Victor suddenly felt something, not like a physical feeling. It was more of a natural feeling of survival. He looked around, he couldn't see anything, he turned

around. Edna had her arm around Francis and he was limping. The dogs had brutally torn themselves into him.

He was losing a lot of blood. But they had done what they could do to make sure that the bleeding had stopped.

Francis and Edna were slowing the rest of the group down, they knew that. But she couldn't leave him. That seemed wrong, even after what he had done to her!

"Come on," she said as she tried to avoid stabbing him in the spine with her kitchen knife.

"I...I...I don't think...I can...continue...I'm so hot!"

"What? Francis! It's freezing!"

Francis then started to unbutton his jacket as he muttered, "I'm burning up!"

He then untied the rope and slipped his jeans off. He tore them off and took off one of his boots in the process. He was now wearing his thin long-sleeved t-shirt and his underwear. Edna shouted "Francis! Stop it! Put your clothes back on!" she was in the process of picking his clothes up when it happened. He let out a cry, his jaw snapped to the side and his left arm bent around his back. His legs bent to the side and she heard his knees and elbows snap. His back arched and he folded inwards.

The entire area around them seemed to shake and rock as the snow exploded behind them. Francis slumped over and landed on top of Edna, knocking the pair of them into the snow. The rest of the group cried out to the two of them. Victor pointed his torch towards them, Edna saw the beam of light slash across her face then disappear.

Something towered over the two of them.

Francis rolled over onto his side and sank into the thick snow. Edna was partly buried as the coldness began to engulf her, she turned onto her back and felt something strong and heavy land on her chest. It struck her with crushing force. She held her chest and felt her ribcage. The bones had been shattered.

She coughed and even in the darkness she saw the white snow turn red where she aimed her mouth.

It didn't hit her for a second time, instead, it grabbed Francis. As it grabbed him and lifted him into the air. He screamed out in pain as he felt something sharp impale his body. It slammed him back down into the snow and Francis let out a loud moan, it lifted him again and this time forced him down into Edna. His back struck Edna in her face and broke her nose and knocked out a few teeth. She swallowed a few but most of them came out of her mouth as they slipped away from her gums.

When it lifted him for the third time his body was consumed by the winter darkness that engulfed the entire group.

Edna could make out his figure, and a second one. It was close to him. But it seemed inhuman, tall slender and screaming! As was Francis! She saw arms reach out and then the snow got thick. She could barely make the two shapes out now. It was just movements. She heard Francis' vocal cords change from a loud groan to a blood-curdling scream, "ARGGGHHHH!"

She heard noises. Oh God the noises! Crushing and snapping noises. Then his scream seemed to die away in the night air.

Edna couldn't move, she was weak and was coughing up blood. She fumbled around for the rope but as felt it, something grabbed her.

He was gentle with me. He loved me. Why? Why did I
lie! I fell! I fucking slipped! He never pushed me! Why?
Now he's gone. And he will never know. I love him!
She let out a cry and a plead. The thing lifted her into the
air and she saw it. She saw what it was, long brown hair
hanging over her cheeks. Eyes torn from the sockets
leaving dark bloody holes. But the head, oh god the
head! It was twisted 360 degrees. The mouth was large
and wide and the girl was at least 8ft tall not to mention
how skinny she was. The girl was her little sister,
Agatha. Edna tried to kick herself free but instead, she
was met with her legs twisting. She felt the skin tear and
the bones break. With this came the fall. Her body hit
the floor and her two legs were consumed by
Agatha. She ate them!
He loves me! Why! Why! No! Please. I don't want
to die! Let me live! Please!
Edna began to drag herself across the snow, Freddie
appeared from the blizzard and he saw Edna crawling
towards him, "Dad..." her hand was out for him to grab
her. He took a step forward then-
Edna felt a cloud of cold darkness cover her body, it was
consuming her. Her body was back in the air but this
time it was different. She felt the jaw begin to sink into
her cheeks, the hot breath on her skull and the wetness
of both saliva and blood touched her skin.
"No...Stop...I..." attempted Edna, her words were weak
and crumbling in her mouth. The jaw snapped shut
around her head. It was getting tight, teeth sinking into
the skin and the bone. She heard the teeth crunch her
skull and one even pierced her cheek, she felt the fang
crush the insides of her mouth but as she was about to
scream her skull burst open inside of Agatha's mouth.

When Edna's limp body slipped from Agatha's grip she turned her attention the last three. She didn't make a sound save for a horrible choking coughing sound. As she lunged forward!

21

The front door burst open with force as the three of them entered the house again. Their bodies weak and cold from the outside world.

She was behind them. They quickly entered the living room and closed the door, they heard Agatha banging on the front door other side. Then the front door was ripped from it's hinges and thrown forward. Agatha entered the house.

Her hands were tapping on the walls. She was hunting them. Victor slowly worked his way into the living room and his parents followed him.

She was there. Standing in the doorway of the dining room. Her head was facing their direction. Yet, she was unaware of their presence. They slowly started to back up. The Brent brothers remained on the floor, the pool of blood had spread out wide. It was Victor who stepped on it by accident. His foot made a squeaking sound. Agatha made her choking coughing sound and threw herself in their direction.

Freddie shouted, "Get in the cellar! Get in the fucking cellar!"

Victor ran over to the door and forced it open, his mum followed him down the stairs and Freddie followed them. He closed the door and locked it from the inside by using the bolt at the top of the door.

When it was over he leaned on the door and cried.

22

Michelle Shallicker was close to death, but the young woman refused to allow death to take her. Yet.

Her hands were tied behind her back and she was attached to the bedpost and her body lay on the floor. She was bloody and beaten.

Thomas was sat on the armchair, his tongue forced out of his mouth and in his hands he took a grip of his crossbow. It was loaded, the bolt was sharp and aimed at her chest. As if ready to fire. All it would take for her to die would be a single pull of the trigger.

He had already shot her six times, her body ached and she was bleeding all over. She was sure he had punctured vital organs save for her heart and lungs. She was bleeding inside and out. If help didn't come soon. She was going to die from blood loss.

Thomas was not himself, he had transformed into a monster. It was the only word she could use to describe him. A monster. His body was twisted and his eyes were cold and dead looking, like marbles.

She had only tried to escape once but that lead to being shot and caught. Thomas had nearly killed Edna and Freddie too!

Several thoughts were washing around her head at this moment, she wanted to escape again and head downstairs. But she had heard noises, screams, the sound of windows smashing and heavy bangs. She heard screams outside too. She was sure that no one else was alive. She was alone. She was alone with insanity.

The second thought disturbed her a lot more than the first for some reason.

She might have to kill Thomas.

He wasn't himself any more, but she knew he was still

there. He had to be, she heard him. His voice was dark and cold but when he really spoke to her. He sounded terrified. She could never live with herself for doing that. But she knew that the real Thomas would be a rest. For now, she shook that thought away and focused mostly on the first one. To escape and head outside, the family could be alive for all she knew. Some of them could be dead. Or all of them could be dead...

That was not her normal way of thinking, Michelle was a level headed girl and could keep her wits about her. But now her life was on the line, her lover had a crossbow pointed at her heart!

And the temperature was dropping fast, it would only be a matter of time before she was killed.

That was not an option. She would not die!

Her hands squirmed but Thomas had used a belt and made sure she was tied to the end of the bed tightly. She thought about possibly lifting the bed with her feet then slipping herself out. She had tried it but was only met with immense pain all over her body. Thomas had left three bolts in her body. He had another four bolts by his side plus one in the notch.

She felt like if the evil side of him wanted her dead, he would have done it by now. Why hadn't he?

Was the real Thomas stopping him from killing her?

Or was he keeping her alive for another reason?

Does he know the truth?

If he does, he might want it.

She had heard stories of people draining her ability by torture. In the past, if you were found to be a telepath or possess mind-reading abilities you would have been tortured until it was either gone or the subject died.

The most recent case happened in 1954.

A young boy was just 14 years old. His mind had the power of a telepath, he used it to cheat in a test in school. He also used it to read his bullies minds and calm them down, he gained friends and became popular. No one could bully sweet Edward Peters.

Then he was found dead in a forest. He was tied to a tree, beaten, abused, bleeding, his arms broken, his left eye removed and his knees smashed apart with rocks. If his power was taken it was unknown.

But whatever took his power, whatever it was. It was back and it was now tearing the farm apart. Reaching up, ripping and tearing into the Martin family.

In truth, Michelle Shallicker didn't know the severity of the situation. She didn't know the macabre deaths that befell Agatha, Richard, Hugo, Francis and Edna.

She also had no idea that the outside temperature was that of the Arctic during the winter. Unlike Francis, Michelle was not suffering from hypothermia. Upstairs was warmer than anywhere in the house.

Michelle, however, was shivering, her dress was not made for the winter months and she was really cold and-

"I'm going to make this easy for you Michelle Shallicker. As you are aware I can deliver painful blows to your body. I know you do not wish for more pain to be inflicted upon you. But I will if you do not give me what I want. I need your power to fuel me. Give it to me. It will not kill you. So I wouldn't worry about that. But it will weaken you. Once I have what I want I will leave you and your lover alone. He too will be weak. Close to death, I might add so...MICHELLE...IGNORE HIM...HE'S LYING...RUN...YOU NEED TO GO! Silence!"

"Thomas?" said Michelle with empathy.

"GO! YOU NEED TO MOVE!"

Thomas lunged forward, he threw the crossbow on the floor and he hit the floor hard. He dragged himself across the floorboards. But it was fighting his movements. He quickly reached upwards and smashed his head into the already broken mirror.

Two screams exploded from his mouth, one sounded as if it was an echo but she knew both sounds came from his mouth.

The real Thomas was partly in control, he said, "MICHELLE...I'M SORRY...I LOVE YOU!"

He reached into the top drawer and pulled out a wooden sewing needle. He forced it towards his neck but the other hand grabbed his wrist.

What Michelle was witnessing was strange, it was as if Thomas was fighting himself.

The hand was forcing the wrist away, the sewing needle was close to becoming forced deep in his throat.

Michelle screamed, "Thomas! No! Please!" she tried to free herself but her body felt weak. Blood began to seep out of her wounds again. As put pressure of them.

She slipped to the side, forcing a crossbow bolt deep into her shoulder. The fletcher was now touching her skin and she let out a cry.

Thomas continued his self fight.

The hand pushed and pushed but Thomas was winning. He then felt the prick of the needle starting to dig into his skin. One final push and-

SNAP!

CRACK!

"ARGGHHH OH...ARGGHH...ARGHH!"

His left arm twisted a full 90 degrees, snapping the

bone. His hand let the sewing needle go and he looked at his arm. Looking at how his hand was now close to his waist. Tears streamed down his cheeks.

"Michelle? I am more than aware that this man loves you. And you don't want to get hurt and you don't want him to get hurt. But believe me when I say this. I can inflict pain on you, and I can inflict even greater pain on Thomas. You saw how I broke his arm without touching him. Now I need you to give me your telepathic ability."

All whilst the man was talking, Michelle heard the cries of Thomas deep in his mouth. His cries of pain and his cries of suffering. He never said a single word as the man spoke. He continued, "You have a power that is not of this world. A human cannot fathom the true power of a telepathic ability. You use it for worthless things. Cheating on a test. Guessing which direction a stranger is going on the path. Or what meat someone wants at your father's butchers. You do not deserve such power!"

He reached out for Michelle, his cold hands grabbed her by the neck and he opened his mouth. His cold lips slipped over hers and she felt his tongue slip deep into her throat. She felt it go down and down.

She began to choke. She would have coughed if she could but the tongue only continued to go down and down. She felt around, she had no choice. She had to do it!

She grabbed the bolt from her calf and tore it free, blood squirted from the wound and onto the floor. Michelle lifted the bolt as her eyes began to roll backwards.

She drove it into his side, she ripped it out and did it again this time a little higher. She felt the tongue slip out of her mouth and he pulled away, she screamed, "Fuck you!" before driving the bolt into his chest. She then lifted her legs and kicked him in the face. She felt his body stumble backwards, she managed to lift the bed with the adrenaline boost and threw herself forward. She rose quickly and stumbled out of the room. She couldn't go anywhere. Michelle headed for Thomas' bedroom. She threw open the door and limped inside. There was nowhere to hide, "I know where you are Michelle!" cried Thomas.

The bed!

Michelle knelt and dragged herself under the bed, she rolled on her stomach, hands over her mouth. Her body was aching and her weight was causing the bolts deeper and deeper into her body. She wanted to cry out. But that meant she would be found. Thomas then entered the room.

Just for a split second everything went silent and all Michelle could think was, I'm going to die today.

23

Michelle held her breath.

She saw as Thomas dragged his feet across the floor, watching him as he slowly began to walk around the bed. She looked across the floor, there was no blood trail. He could leave once he realised she wasn't here. She felt dampness underneath her body. When the bolts were pushing their way through her body.

She then realised something that terrified her.

The human body was just a sack of blood. All it took was one stab and it would pour out unless it was stopped. She was like a bag of water being stabbed with pins. Michelle then saw a blood puddle forming under her chest and it was working its way to the end of the

bed. She quickly used her arms to wipe it up.
She feared she was going to bleed out.
She had in fact lost two pints of blood. Although she
was weak, she was still okay and could lose a little
more. Michelle managed to stop the flow by turning
onto her side.
Her mind was suddenly taken back slightly.
It was around a year ago. Herself and Thomas were
going through a rough patch. They were a young couple
and arguments were going to happen, they were
unavoidable. This argument, however, it was different
from the other ones. It had caused a crack in their
relationship, it had started over a missed phone call.
The week it had occurred, Thomas was so busy with the
work that his dad has assigned to him. He had spent
most of Friday slaughtering pigs with the captive bolt
pistol. One would come near him and he would force a
bolt through its brain. Time only went on.
Thomas had missed phone call after phone call, it even
came to the point where Michelle came to the farm
herself. Although now it's clear that she had overreacted.
And this is what lead to the problems. She was prone to
overreacting. This was only clear on the six-month
mark, Thomas hated this and would sometimes shout at
her. She knew he was busy at times so she could let it
slide. When it occurred on Friday's and Saturday's
(Thomas' days off) she would get upset. Unless he told
her. This time he forgot to tell her that his dad wanted
him to work in the slaughter room for one night. Hugo
had caught the flu and Thomas was asked to work for a
few hours. He did have a date planned with Michelle for
that evening and to even stay with her that night in
Orington and return Sunday morning for work.

Thomas had been busy and stressed during the week and had simply forgotten about the date they had planned two weeks prior. Not to mention forgetting to tell her about working late. That night when she came she shouted at him, calling him out for ignoring her. She had initially presumed he was cheating on her. But after searching the barn she knew that was not the case.

The case was Thomas was keeping things from her. Whether it be working late or as Michelle worded it, "Other things that keep you happy!"

They broke up for a month, Thomas no longer joined his dad with deliveries at the butchers and Michelle didn't hand Freddie any letters. Instead, Victor or Edna would join him for the trip.

His dad didn't mind him not showing up for the trips as it seemed a little intimidating. Freddie had spoken to Patrick about it but Michelle didn't say much about Thomas in the passing weeks. Neither of them cared, or they were hiding the truth behind their eyes.

The pair eventually met up by accident in Orington. Thomas was just walking through the park when he saw Michelle walking her dog. At first, he wanted to ignore her and she later admitted she wanted to do the same. But something in him convinced him to talk to her, he truly loved her and didn't want to lose her over a petty argument as such as this one. He had run over to her and explained himself, he asked her to think about it and if she wanted to go back to normal. Call him tonight before 10:00 pm.

He waited in the living room for over an hour, not moving away from the telephone, then at 10:30 pm. The phone rang, he wanted to pick it up straight away. But he waited and after three rings, he snatched the

phone up and the pair spoke for two hours.
They got back together and the incident was forgotten.
Until now. It was strange how she thought of it whilst
she hid under a bed, her body punctured and bleeding.
Not to mention she was partially blind due to losing her
glasses when Thomas punched her in the nose earlier.
Michelle looked around the room, she didn't see his feet
or hear him crawl on the bed in wait for her. She waited
for what seemed like an hour then slowly began to pull
herself out from under the bed. She opened the drawer
and removed a small pocket knife, she unfolded the
blade and held it tightly. She knew Thomas had a
revolver in one of his drawers, she looked for it but only
found the bullets. She grunted and slammed the drawer
shut. Once she reached the door to leave she heard
heavy breathing as if someone was having a panic
attack. She lifted her head and there on the ceiling was
Thomas. He was looking down at her, his back had split
open and spines had torn out of his flesh to keep his
grip.
In his hands, he held the crossbow. It was pointed
towards her chest again.
Michelle cried and said, "Please...don't...Thomas...I
know you're still there. Please...I love you."
For a second Thomas seemed to change, he lowered the
crossbow. But he raised it again and pulled the trigger.
The bolt hit her in her stomach. She grabbed it and the
force of it knocked her off her feet. She hit her head on
the wall and cried out in pain. She held the fletcher, she
knew better than to pull it out. Thomas slowly slipped
onto the floor. He was no longer what could be
described as human. His back was covered in spines and
his face had changed. It was grotesque. His eyes were

dead and staring. He lifted his body and Michelle could only scream, she quickly dragged herself onto the landing and Thomas followed her.

24

In the cellar Freddie, Gwenda and Victor had all wrapped themselves up in blankets. The temperature in here had dropped drastically and only continued to drop.

They had gathered in the corner, Gwenda was hugging Victor whilst crying and Freddie was stood up.

They had not exchanged any words since they got in here. They only shivered and hugged one another.

Agatha was still upstairs, they heard her what they thought was the kitchen. She was probably eating the remains of the dogs. Then Victor spoke he kept his voice down they had learnt that Agatha hunted by sound, "There must be a way out."

No one said anything, instead, Freddie sat himself down at the base of the stairs and leaned his head on the wall. Thought after thought raced through his head.

Victor looked around the room, it was quite big for a cellar with crates and boxes stuffed into the corner. Along with the Christmas decorations and tools were hooked onto the wall by screws that Freddie had drilled there years ago.

He then spotted the window in the far corner of the room, it wasn't that big. Victor used to hide inside of here during the summer when he had water fights with his siblings. Running around the grass with their bare feet. The smell of fresh lemonade and fresh fruits as the apple trees exploded with colour and sweetness.

Victor found himself smiling at the thought.

Seeing his siblings run towards him with water pistols, their laughter, their cries of joy and the conversations they had as they shared a jug of fresh lemonade.
The wall of reality hit him.
They were dead.
He was the last one of the Martin children. His older brother was insane from what Freddie had told him.
Firing a crossbow at his sister and dad.
Victor was the last one and it didn't only scare him, it upset him. He saw all of it. He saw how Edna has her skull crushed. He saw how Heather was torn apart.
He saw what Agatha had become.
He didn't want that for anyone else.
Victor was not ready to die, not by something that was hunting them all down and killing them!
Then his mum said, "How many bullets do you have darling?"
"I have four left. Why?"
Gwenda sighed and said, "We aren't going to get out of here. You saw what she did to Edna, heard what happened to Francis. Saw what Agatha, Thomas, Richard and Hugo became. Saw how our baby girl was torn apart. We can make it quick," she offered her hand for the revolver.
"You want us to shoot ourselves?" exclaimed Freddie.
"We don't really have a choice, Freddie! I don't want my death to be violent!"
"No! We are not going to do that!"
"Freddie, please. We can hug each other and lie down and pull the trigger!"
"I don't want to die," said Victor tearfully.
"You won't feel a-"
"Shut up woman! Stop scaring him. We are not going to

kill ourselves. We are Martin's. We stick together. We will escape this farm if it kills me!"

BANG!

It was the cellar door. Agatha had heard the commotion and she wanted to come in. Freddie quickly hugged Victor and Gwenda, he held their mouths shut with his hands and the three of them sat down under the cellar stairs. They heard her scratching and clawing on the door as if she testing it. They knew she was more than capable of breaking that door down if she wanted too. They saw how she ripped the front door from its hinges. They waited, they were quiet. Then they heard her run across the floor and into another room.

Freddie removed his hands and said, "We need to be quiet," his voice was low, "Gwenda, get that thought of your head now. It's not going to be an option."

Gwenda didn't say any more. Instead, she hugged her knees and placed her head on top of them.

For the first time in his life, Victor Martin wanted to pray. Pray to God for his and his families survival. Pray for God before the devil dragged them into hell, he had a feeling he was in hell. And this was his punishment. Being punished for more of what he was rather than what he had done. What else had the family done?

He checked his watch for some reason, the face was cracked and ice was forming around the edges, he heard it ticking. The time was 6:45 pm.

He looked up at the window in the corner, it was dark outside and ice was forming on the glass. The glass started to frost over and was spreading like a fungus. Then Victor had an idea.

"I have an idea, could we not use the window to get out?

It's fairly big."
"Vic, me and your mum aren't getting through that," said
Freddie as he got a closer look at the window.
Victor thought again then said, "Maybe I could."
"Don't be stupid buddy. If she sees you she'll kill you,"
said Freddie as he placed his hand on Victor's back. But
Victor was determined to convince his parents
otherwise, "Well, maybe I could go through it. I can run
to the truck. Smash the window or something to make a
loud noise. It should draw her outside, I can hide under
the porch then we all make a run for it through the forest
or something," he said with excitement.
Freddie thought about it then said, "That might actually
work. But you need to be very careful."
"No! He isn't going," said Gwenda.
"We don't have a choice darling. We either get killed by
the thing upstairs. Or we freeze to death," said Freddie
as he placed his hands on his wife's shoulders.
"I...I can't lose another child...it might just kill me," she
said softly."
"Darling. Please. We don't have a choice. Vic is our only
chance of survival now. I can put him on my shoulders
and he can squeeze through the window. Make some
noise and hide. We can then make a run for it through
the back door to the woods. Together," he smiled at her.
But she did not return a smile, instead, she pushed his
hands away and said, "I will not lose any more of my
children. Too many of my children have died tonight. I
saw their eyes. Their beautiful faces. I saw one of them
go mad and shoot his sister and dad with a crossbow. I
saw what our farm handlers had become. My daughter
had to kill it with her dad before it killed anyone! I saw
our daughter get mauled to death by three dogs that we

loved and cherished. I saw my other daughter come back her body twisted and contorted. I saw my eldest daughter get her head crushed by a monster that I once loved and called my daughter. That I once called Agatha," she started to tear up, "So no. I don't want Victor to go. He is the only thing that we have left Freddie. I don't understand how you could want him to just go out there and risk his life. His short life. He's been through hell. You've been through hell. Michelle and Thomas have been through hell. I can't let him go. He's my last child that hasn't been taken from me. Please let me go. I can do it."

"Gwenda," said Freddie as he took his wife by the hands, "I understand. We have all been through hell. We will not be trapped in this predicament of who will go and who will stay. Victor is going, end of story. Come on Vic I'll help you up. But be quiet," he kept his voice down all the way through and even tiptoed over to the window. Victor looked at his mother then to his father he didn't want to hurt her, but he also didn't want her to go out there. It was far too dangerous for any of them. If Agatha had somehow worked her way outside he could easily get by her.

"Mum, I can do it. I promise I'll be standing at the top of those stairs and we can make a run for it to the forest," said Victor as he tried to hold back the tears.

He thought long and hard about it before actually walking over to Freddie, he stood on his hand and pulled himself up to the small ledge that stuck out. He pressed his free hand on the glass and the window was pushed open. Some snow was pushed out of the way and the cold breeze of the evening air blew into the small gap. Victor was about to press his head through the gap when he heard something, it came from the far left of the window. He looked across the land and saw Heather. He looked down at Freddie with fear in his eyes and looked back at Heather, she was crawling across the snow and then started to walk up the wall. She was like a skinless spider, her skin was pale, her eyes completely black and an extra pair of arms and legs had grown out of her body. Her throat continued to bleed but not in large amounts as it had done beforehand. Victor looked closely at her mouth, it was no longer human. No lips, teeth or gums. Her mouth had turned into two large fangs, black fangs with something dripping from the sharp tips.

Victor gasped at the sight and pulled himself backwards. He made sure that he didn't kick his dad in the face in the process of him falling. He hit the floor with a heavy thud and his parents looked at him.

"What was it?" whispered Freddie.

"Heather," said Victor as he ran his hands over his face.

"Heather? What do you mean?" asked Gwenda as she got closer to her son.

"She's one of them. She's like Agatha, Richard and Hugo. She isn't human any more."

"Shit," said Freddie.

Gwenda collapsed to her knees and started to cry but she didn't make a sound apart from the odd gasp for her breath. All Freddie and Victor could do was look at her with the same thought in their minds, that was until she spoke and said, "This is my fault. God. He is punishing me for my sins. For my horrible sins of lust. This is what God does to sinners. It's my fault and I am so sorry Freddie, Victor."

"What do you mean by sins of lust?" asked Freddie.

"I...I love you, Freddie. I don't know why I did it,"

"You've cheated on me?"

"Mum, Dad. Please we need to-"

"Shut up Victor! I need to know," cried Freddie.

"I love you. Please you need to understand,"

"What do you mean? Tell me," he grabbed her shoulders tightly.

"I...I was lost. My mind was messed up. From Toby's death. Please just understand me. I will understand your anger. I was having sex with Hugo. Ever since he started here,"

"That was over four years ago," he almost shouted his words.

"Please. I'm sorry. I need to tell you now."

"You should have taken that secret to your rotting grave. That's why you wanted us to commit suicide!" his voice was breaking out into shouting now.

Victor pressed himself against the wall, trying to not make a sound or get involved in his parent's outburst.

"What other filthy secrets have you been keeping from me!" he shouted.

"Please. Understand me-"

"Understand! How the fuck can I understand this! You fucking whore! I loved you! We had five children together!"

"Four," she corrected him and did so without hesitation as if she was ready to tell him.

Victor and Freddie looked at her deeply in her eyes, "What!"

"Heather. She's Hugo's daughter. Not yours," she was crying now tears poured out of her eyes and down her cheeks.

"How could you? Was I not good enough for you!"

"I love you!"

"Don't give me none of that shit! How dare you sleep with him. He was a child! How fucking dare you!"

"I know! I know! And I'm sorry! I still love you!"

Freddie threw her across the basement, she hit the wall hard and bounced from it before hitting the floor hard.

"You don't love me! You fucked some boy! Did you not think about how that would make me feel?"

"Freddie. Please! It's your fault!" she shouted with anger.

"Me! How the fuck is it me?" he walked over to her and grabbed her by the chest and slammed her into the wall once more.

"You spent all your time reading and getting drunk! I needed you! Hugo was my...my medication...he was gentle with me...and soft..." she stopped herself from speaking, she had already said too much.

"You what? You love him more than me!"

He pulled his hand free from her and turned away. His eyes started to tear up.

Then he removed the revolver from his belt, he lifted it and aimed it at her, "I'm going to kill you!"

"What! No! Freddie, please don't do this!"

She saw as the .357 revolver was pointed at her skull. He pulled back the hammer and was ready to fire.

"You deserve to die for what you've put me and the family through. I cried over a child that wasn't even mine! I know I haven't been the best. But at least I wasn't fucking some young girl in Orington! No matter how depressed I was!"

"I'm sor-"

"No, you're not!"

He made sure the revolver was pointed at her skull, one

bullet. That's all it would take, "You wanted this. Remember! You wanted to die!"

"Freddie! Please!"

The fear coming off his body and felt the pain and torture coming off of hers. He lowered the gun and said, "I can't. I can't do it!"

Victor let out a deep breath and so did Gwenda, but it all happened so fast. From the open window, they heard a loud hissing sound, Heather's four arms wrapped around the window frame and she dragged herself inside. Her teeth clattered together in her mouth and she let gasping sound she turned her head 90 degrees and looked at Freddie she then crawled down the wall and everyone pulled themselves backwards.

Victor quickly hid himself under the stairs and Gwenda dragged herself up but slipped and landed on her left arm, her bone broke and it forced itself out of her elbow. She was about to let out a scream but Heather had already seen what had happened to Gwenda and how weak she had become, she ran over to her and jumped on top of her mum. Her hands pinned Gwenda down, she began to bite into Gwenda's arm that she used to shield herself from the bites.

Gwenda cried out for help but all Freddie did was watch from a distance. Victor took out his kitchen knife and ran to Gwenda.

Heather opened up her mouth and started to bite Gwenda on her face rapidly, each bite injecting a fatal poison into her bloodstream. She lifted her hand again to shield her face but that only made things worse, Heather continued to bite her mother's flesh all whilst Freddie stood near the stairs and watched on as Gwenda was being bitten to death. Victor stood over the two of them

not knowing where to stab in case he hit his mum.
"I don't wanna-"
She was going to say die but Heather's fangs bite her on
her tongue. She lifted Heather into the air as a thick
foam, like cake batter started to form in her mouth and
spill from the sides. Victor then brought the knife down
into Heather's back. She made a loud hissing sound and
jumped onto the wall, Victor was about to stab her in the
neck but her fangs pointed outwards. Hot venom was
spat from the fangs, the first streak hit Victor on his
shoulder, it mostly stung but was no worse than a burn
from hot water. But the second one hit him in his left
eye. Victor screamed out in pain and Freddie made his
move. He grabbed Victor and checked his left eye, it had
gone bloodshot and the skin around was peeling and
blistering. His eye started to turn red as it lost its colour.
The two of them hadn't noticed the state of Gwenda.
She lay on her back, her good hand wrapped around her
throat that was now fat and swollen from the venom.
Victor then noticed his mum, he ran to her with pain and
tears in his eyes. He knelt beside her and grabbed her
hand. She tried to speak but she started to choke. Her
skin turned black where Heather had bitten her and her
veins started to push their way out of her skin. A terrible
mixture of blood, foam and the egg white fluid was
pouring down the sides of her mouth. Victor saw the fear
in her eyes as her hands clawed at her throat, her neck
hardened like stone and her nails dug into her flesh
making it bleed. Victor held her hand and tapped it. It
seemed to be the only thing he could do to make it stop.
But he knew that she was going to die.
It took a full four minutes until Gwenda Martin had
succumbed to suffocation. Victor knew she was dead

when her hand slipped from his.

He then turned to face his dad and said, "Why? Why did you just stand there?"

Freddie didn't reply, instead, he sat on the stairs and ran his hands over his face.

Then he started to cry as he whispered, "I'm sorry..."

3

1

In his mind, his sanity had crumbled and cracked over the last few hours. It was ever since he had that dream. Now he was nothing more than a prisoner. A prisoner in his own mind as it was slowly taken over by an unknown entity. He had not seen it. But he felt it, the coldness that started to consume him. He had fallen ill yesterday morning. His body felt slow and weak, his head pounded and his heart rate began to increase. He felt every inch of pain that the entity had endured upon him.

It all went downhill when Michelle had taken him into the bathroom for the final time. He felt cold, isolated and he couldn't stop vomiting in the toilet bowl.

All of a sudden the pain became to that of tolerable to completely unbearable. His body began to twist and transform, he remembered his body folding in half, his head slammed into the floor and his eyes rolled back. He saw Michelle scramble backwards and climb out of the bathroom. She must have been so scared and he couldn't do a thing about it but lie there and watch her.

He wanted to reach out to her and tell her everything was going to be okay. But it wasn't.

Things were never going to be okay again.

He knew he wasn't himself when he started to snap at her, his mood swings changed from anger, fear and regret. He never thought he would raise a hand to her. Never! But last night he had done more than raise a hand to her, he had tortured her. He had cut her open, shot her with a crossbow and had beaten her senseless.

The worst thing he had done was slice between her legs with the cut-throat razor. He had pinned her down.

She screamed for him to stop as he unfolded the blade, it was sharp and ready to cut. He pressed it into her thigh and began to saw at her skin. Then he moved into the middle of her legs, blood covered his hands and she screamed out in terror.

He had his own fair share of pain.

He attempted to commit suicide with a sewing needle he found in his mum's dressing table. But as he tried to stick it through his neck, his arm snapped at the elbow. He felt it. He heard it.

But what made matters was he was trapped in himself, his eyes became his windows as he watched his own hands torture Michelle. Each time he lifted the crossbow or unfolded the cutthroat he felt regret and guilt consume him. He could only watch as madness took its toll before him. Watch as his girlfriend of two years screamed for him to stop. Screamed that she loved him and all he could do was watch. He needed to fight back. It was his own body!

He couldn't let this continue any longer.

He felt as if he was drunk walking through the darkness, his hands feeling around for something. Anything, but all he felt was the coldness.

Mum, dad, Agatha, Edna, Victor?

His family, what had happened to them throughout the day. He remembered shooting Edna and his dad. Did he kill them? He hoped he didn't. He prayed to God that his family were still alive. He knew Agatha was missing and if his assumption was correct, his baby sister was dead. He felt something every time something horrible happened. He somehow managed to get into the entities thoughts. It had a similar brain structure to that of a human but was far more superior than anything Thomas could have ever imagined. It was dire. It was insane. It was madness. It was monstrous.

He could see what happened to Agatha, her small body swaying from side to side. Her arms reaching up for the hands that grasped around her ankles. Or the jaws? Agatha let out a cry and...and..it...oh god!

He could think no more, the more he dug into its mind the more he got lost. It was like being lost in a dark forest. His hands continuing to work around, feeling through the matter, once he found a pressure point it would cry out and Thomas was back in control. He shouted for Michelle to run, to getaway. She knew it was him when the real Thomas spoke. He saw how her face had changed into a realisation that her boyfriend was still there. Still alive.

When he followed her into the bedroom he just wanted to hold himself back. To do something so little, he might be able to save her. To get her out of the situation. He knew she had gone under the bed, but he wasn't sure if the other thing had noticed this. So he kept it under lock and key, but it broke the lock and played games with her.

Once the entity dragged his body upon the ceiling he was sure it had worked her out. It moved quickly and without hesitation, to stop him from saying anything it broke his jaw. He felt it slip away from the rest of his skull and the pain was horrendous. It shot through him like a hot bullet. He even tried to make a noise but as she crawled out the sound must have scared her. She let out a gasp and made a run for the door.

He felt helpless that he couldn't do anything to help her. He had to sit still and watch as the terror unfolded in front of him.

Thomas didn't want to give up, he couldn't let this being take over him and hurt the one he loved. He felt himself starting to disappear, his body was fusing with the evil within. And when it consumed him he would be gone and never seen again.

That was his biggest fear. Being taken from those he loved. He knew his family were dying. He felt it now. It was within his thoughts. The tongues spoke to him. Webbing words around him. Creating a world that he never knew or wanted to exist. It was there. Reaching out, clawing and scratching towards him. Once it took hold, it filled his soul with what had really happened to his family. The two Brent brothers, their final moments as they both screamed. Richard reaching his hands out as the thing grabbed him and tore him open. Hugo, he cried out and his words stopped. His head rolled from his body. Heather, poor little Heather. She felt nothing but sadness and a feeling of terror as those dog's jaws snapped closed around her head and shoulders.

Edna and her boyfriend who she truly loved, she never

admitted to it. At first, he didn't think he liked his siblings or even knew who they were. But now he can, he can see inside of them. Edna loved Francis. She never told him before he was crushed by Agatha, she came back as some horrific creature. And Edna, she tried to fight back. The blizzard, the sounds of her lover being killed and then her sister tearing into her. It was more than enough pain for her to endure. Thomas never wished for this.

Love was a powerful thing. It's what makes us human. It's something we can give as well as receive. It was something that kept people together. It was the only thing giving Thomas Martin hope. He was going to make it through this ordeal, he was going to get himself and his family out of this. He just needed to fight back. It was love.

As soon as he thought of it, the feeling of being trapped began to ease and he felt pain. Not his own. But the pain of the thing as it screamed and began to fall apart...

2

Michelle Shallicker had somehow scrambled onto the third floor of the farmhouse. She had never seen the third floor to the house and was not use to which door lead to what. At first, when she reached the stairs Thomas had fired the crossbow. Luckily it struck the wall beside her. Leaving an antenna sticking out of the wallpaper. Michelle reached the top of the stairs and tried the first door, only to find it was locked. She tried the door to the right and that was locked too. When she reached the door on the left it was an empty room with a window overlooking the left side of the farm. She could hear Thomas as he started to run up the stairs. His feet hammering on the stairs and his voice getting louder and louder. She had nothing to defend herself with, she needed to find something and fast. She ran into one of the rooms, almost knocking the door down.

Her hands scrambled over the top of the tables and chest of drawers as she felt for something to use. She pulled open the top drawer and began to quickly look around. Her hand pushing things out of the way. As she was determined to find something sharp or blunt. There was mostly old letters, papers, documents and even a box of matches.

Then her hand slipped over something, she pulled it from the papers and held it into the air. It was a screwdriver, the tip was thin but it looked sharp enough to stab with. It would have to do!

Michelle leaned on the chest of drawers and braced herself for Thomas. Waiting for him to break the door down or enter and shoot her with the crossbow. She could hear him, his feet on the floor and his hands shaking the door handles. She prayed that it would not come to the worst of it, she didn't know if she could bring herself to kill him. Thomas was her one and only, but she knew the real Thomas was long gone. It was more than clear that the real Thomas was dead.

She held the screwdriver with her left hand and used the weight of the drawers to support her injured body.

She heard him at the door now, his hand clawing at the handle and she heard something heavy tap on the wooden door. He still had that damn crossbow!

Michelle kept her mouth closed. She was still debating if she should go through with her plan. Her plan of killing him. His mind was gone but his body remained.

She waited. And waited.

For some reason he didn't try and open the door any more, instead, he continued to walk. He didn't speak and he moved onto another room. What was he doing?

She relaxed a little and her grip loosened on the screwdriver. She slowly began to sit down in front of the chest of drawers. Her face ached and her body was starting to hurt more.

She was going to kill him. She didn't want it to walk around the house, dragging Thomas' body around as if it belonged to it. She just needed to rest, yes that was all she needed. To rest and to wait.

But wait for what? To kill? Or to die?

She wasn't going to do die, she knew that. She wasn't going to allow it. She gritted her teeth and stood up, her pain tried to bring her down. She wasn't going to allow that to happen. Michelle limped her way across the room, she had taken much tighter grip of the screwdriver now. She looked into the hallway, it was dark but her eyes had adjusted to it. And a cold breeze began to fill the small hallway. She looked up at the fourth door. It was slightly elevated and the way to access it was some stairs. It was used as the attic for the Martin's. It was a place she never wanted to go inside. It was around the size of an average bedroom. It had three windows. A circular window in the middle top and two large ones on the left and the right. She could see that when she came onto the farm. It seemed too open.

Michelle took a deep breath and began to walk up the stairs, each one creaked after each step she took. Her heart rate began to increase. And she didn't know if Thomas was up here. It was the only logical place it could have taken him.

BANG!

She lifted her head and looked into the room.

The door was closed and she heard Thomas running around inside, he was running into things. Knocking them over and screaming, "GET OUT OF MY HEAD!"

"Thomas..." she whispered as she was tempted to open the door. What was he doing? Was he winning?

She hoped he was.

Then he hit the door. She saw it shake and wobble.

"GO! I..SHE'S MINE...NOT YOURS!"

Yes, he was winning!

She couldn't open the door, if he was distracted he could be taken again.

She pressed her ear on the door and listened carefully to what was happening behind the closed door. The noises began to grow louder and louder. She slowly pulled herself backwards and listened closely to what Thomas was saying, "NO!...YOU'RE NOT STRONGER THAN MEEEEE!"

Then inside the room went dead.

Michelle waited and waited until she could wait no more. She slowly opened the door and then it hit her, the cold gush of wind whipped her in the chest. It almost knocked her back. Once it was gone she pushed open the door all the way and looked inside. Boxes were sprawled all across the floor, the wallpaper had been ripped from the walls in some places.

And Thomas, he was lying against the wall. His nose was bloody and his skin was covered in sweat. But he no longer looked disfigured. He looked his handsome self again. Michelle limped over to him. She grabbed his shoulders and shook him gently and said, "Thomas. Thomas..."

His eyes slowly opened and his lips formed a smile, his

arms reached out and he hugged her. He pulled her body towards him and cried in her shoulder. He was mumbling some words to her, he squeezed her tightly unaware he was hurting her. He then said, "I am so sorry. I am so sorry. I never meant to hurt you," his soft lips kissed her cheek like he used to.

She kissed him on his lips and said, "It's okay. It's okay. Your back now. It's okay."

She never let him go, she couldn't let him go. He was back and it was all back to normal.

"I'm so glad you are back Thomas. I missed you. I missed you so much," said Michelle with tears in her eyes as she continued to hug him.

"You are everything to me, Michelle. I will never hurt you like I have done tonight. I...I couldn't control it. It was taking over," he couldn't finish his sentence. He was too choked with sadness and guilt to even speak.

She hugged him and brought his head to her chest and hushed him, "It's okay darling...It's okay..."

Her body ached more, she had to pull herself away and when he saw what he had done to her he knew he was more than a bad person.

He was about to speak when he said, "Can you smell that?"

She sniffed the air, it smelled like ember she slowly started to stand. And she sniffed the air once more just to confirm what she smelled earlier was true. And it was. She could smell burning ember.

"Burning?" said Thomas.

"Yes...what's happening?"

"I'm not sure maybe-"

The house shook violently and as it shook Michelle almost fell to the floor. But instead, she just lost her balance. Smoke quickly began to drift from under the door and fill the room. They heard the flames crackle and felt it as the building began to shake. The two of them looked at one another.

It was an explosion, and it felt as if it had happened in the kitchen...

3

"What do we do?" asked Michelle as she sat next to him.

"I...I'm...not sure..."

Michelle pulled herself closer to him, it could be the last time they did this so she said, "It's been a funny day hasn't it," she gave a dry laugh and so did Thomas before he kissed her forehead and nodded with agreement, "It has Michelle."

She pressed her head on his shoulder and he wrapped his arms around her. She didn't know it, but she was slowly bleeding to death. Thomas was weak and with the smoke, he would slowly suffocate. Then a thought entered his head.

From his pocket, he took out the cut-throat razor and held it up in between the two of them. She looked at him and he looked at her. Their eyes locked together and he said,

"I don't want us to be in any more pain, Michelle."

"I know. Neither do I," she held his hand that held the razor.

"Who should go first?"

"I will," she said as she reached out for the razor, "Will it hurt?" she asked as she took the blade from his grasp.

"It will for a second, then we can both wait. Die with each other. With the smoke, we will probably pass out

first. It will be quick and I'll make it as painless as possible."
She could only nod as she wiped the tears away.
BANG! BANG! BANG!
The door began to shake, from the darkness, fingers began to creep through the gaps in the door. There were too many fingers there that belonged to a set of hands. Then the door opened, a hand wrapped around the door. Followed by another, and another and another and another and another...
The two of them looked at each other quickly, she dug the blade deep into her wrist and let out a small gasp. She did the same to the other. Blood dripped down onto her palms. He took the razor from her and slashed downwards on his wrist he cried out and then slashed down deeply with the other. His arms and hands were covered in blood.
The hands continued to claw around the door.
"I love you, Thomas," she said as she leaned towards him.
"I love you too Michelle," his eyes were filled with tears.
Ffftttttt!
Her head snapped back and her eyes rolled back as she slumped backwards. A crossbow bolt had gone through her suprahyoid region and the tip had emerged from the parietal region of her skull. His eyes became waterfalls as he pulled the crossbow away from his lap. He knew it had to one of them who died right away, he had to lie to her to make sure she went through with him. He just wanted to hear those four words once more. He threw the crossbow down and punched the floor. He had killed her instantly. Her body was still and a pool of blood was

forming around her skull.

He looked up at the door and it seemed as if thousands and thousands of hands were reaching out towards him. One grasped his neck and another his arm, they lifted him into the air. He felt them sink into his body, all he could do was groan and cry as they slowly devoured him. His face began to turn purple as the blood got trapped in his face due to how tight the grip was.

Then he saw it's face, OH GOD!

His eyes began to turn red as the veins in his eyeballs began to burst. Blood cried down his face mixing with his tears. His nose began to bleed too and his mouth began to foam up. His body was shaking.

In his final moments, all Thomas Martin could think of was Michelle Shallicker and how much he truly loved the girl...

4

Victor Martin looked at his dad as he sat on the floor at the base of the stairs. In his hand, he held the revolver tightly in his grip. He only had four bullets left still.

Victor had not spoken to him, he didn't want too.

The man had allowed his mum to die, he just stood there and watched as she cried out for help and he let her die! How could he do such a thing?

Victor kept hold of his mum's hand. His grip was strong and her body felt cold. Her eyes were wide and her mouth was foaming. Her throat had swollen to the size of a rugby ball and her arm was also severely swollen. He could see the veins pushing against the flesh. Ready to tear through the paper-thin skin.

She had turned ugly, her face was now that of a hideous ugly monster. He didn't care, Victor still loved her.

His father had done something awful. Something that he could not quite forgive. It was attached to him.

Freddie had lifted his head now and again and had wondered if he should ask Victor to head upstairs with him. Whilst the two of them made a run for it to the forest. The only problem was the blizzard, it could blind them and make them get lost from one another. That had happened before and it had lead to two people being killed, one of whom was his daughter. Freddie refused to give up. He would not allow it.

Victor turned his back on Freddie. He tried to not make any contact with him in any way. Victor had cried more than once since Gwenda had died. He needed to get out of this cellar. Out of this house and as far away as possible. For all, he knew he and his dad could be the only two left standing. He felt like he could no longer trust his dad anymore. He looked back down at his mum and closed his eyes before grabbing a blanket from one of the boxes and placing it over her.

"I should have shot her to end her misery," said Freddie suddenly, "I should have given her what she wanted. She wanted to die."

"You're being selfish! She wanted us to all die together! Not alone! Now, look at her! LOOK AT HER!"

Freddie didn't say anything, he pulled his knees up to his chin and the .357 magnum was placed on top of his knees. He turned the gun around so the barrel was in his hand and the grip was pointed towards Victor. Freddie opened his dry lips and said, "Take it. Take it and go," Freddie waved the gun up and down, "You know how it works don't you? You pull the hammer back and fire." Victor nodded with confusion, he didn't want the gun. He didn't want to hold something that was dangerous.

Something that could kill him.

"Climb out through the window, I'll make as much noise as possible to draw them back inside here. Hopefully, they come. The gun is your way out no matter what in this situation."

Victor didn't once reach his hand out for the revolver, he didn't want to hold it, "Dad...I...no!"

"I can't come with you. I've messed up big time. I let her die. You're right. But let me tell you something before you start accusing me of murdering your mum. Okay?"

"There is nothing you can tell me that will change my mind about this You let her die! Yeah, she messed up. But have you never messed up before?" his voice was getting louder now.

"Think about what you just said, Vic. Your mum was having sex with one of the Brent brothers. She was in a bad place. I was in a bad place. But so was the entire farm. We were in debt. Stresses were piling up and your brother was killed in a tragic accident."

It was the first time the two of them had started to have a conversation about young Toby.

"Toby..." said Victor as if he just remembered him again.

"Yes, Toby. I had taken to the bottle and reading. I was drinking around two bottles of whisky a day. I wasn't supporting your mum in the way I should have. We hardly spoke. We never kissed, hugged or held hands when was in bed. I never told her everything was going to be okay. I was responsible for Toby's death. It was an accident, yes. But I should have been looking at what I was doing. I knew I had hit him when he screamed. I will never forget that scream. I quickly stopped and climbed out, there he was. Tangled in the blades.

I managed to free him, but there was so much blood.
God, there was so much of it. I was covered by the time
your mum came running over. I held Toby for what
seemed like hours. It couldn't have been more for sixty
seconds, Vic. Your mum took his body away from me
and I turned away. I was having a panic attack. I pressed
my hands on the blades of the combine and began to
vomit. Everything went silent. I could hear nothing, not
the sound of your mum screaming or Toby struggling for
breath," Freddie kept his head in his knees he whole
time and Victor listened until he said, "He was still
alive?"
"Yeah, I pretended he died in my arms when I pulled
him out. It seemed to numb the pain. But only numb it. I
knew it was still there. Myself and your mum never
spoke about it. We never had a night where we both sat
down and spoke about his death. For years I said he died
in my arms, when in reality. He died in your mums. She
held him on the floor. Stroking his head and telling him
everything was going to be okay. Whilst she cried. Toby
never spoke. His tongue had been destroyed. When he
died a few minutes later. I knelt by her and we both held
him. We all have regrets Victor, mine is not holding
Toby when he died. And not talking to your mum about
the whole ordeal. I could have saved us both a lot of
pain. Then again it works both ways. She never spoke to
me about it. Then I find out she was sleeping with Hugo
Brent," although there was an almost unbearable amount
of anger building up within him, Freddie Peter Martin
managed to remain calm, "The death of Toby destroyed
this family. We all suffered in our own little ways. You
were a little too young to understand. Thomas and Edna
felt it. I remember when Thomas asked me once at

dinner when was Toby coming back. I couldn't look at him in the eye when I told him. Deep down, I always knew the love between me and your mum was dying. We had six children together. I tried to deny the existence of Toby for many years. But I was a fool for thinking your mum still loved me. She stopped loving me and she fell in love with Hugo. Some child. She lost love for me. But that's not why I let her die, Victor. I let her die because she was threatening to kill us. She wanted me to do a murder-suicide. I couldn't bring myself to kill her in front of you. I knew she was a danger to us when the dogs attacked. She left Heather alone behind the couch. She should have kept hold of her. Now, Heather is dead. When Heather came back I was pleased she went for your mum. I knew she was going to die. I allowed it to happen. And as a result, you got hurt. For that, I will never forgive myself. Love kills you sometimes Victor. Don't fall in love pal. It only breaks you. I don't regret falling for your mum. I had you lot. You are part of me, and that's something that can be never taken away. No matter how angry you get with me. I will always be part of you, Victor. I've lost a great deal tonight. But I haven't lost you. My beautiful baby boy," Freddie placed the revolver down and walked over to him, he knelt beside him and said, "I'm not asking for you to forgive me. You're a young man. You can make up your own mind. But at least consider my story."

"I...I don't know...what to say...it's a lot to take in," said Victor as he ran his hands over his thighs.

"I know. I'm just showing you how awful love can be. Love is a wonderful thing, Victor. But it is also a terrible thing. I hope that when you meet the man of your dreams he treats you right," Freddie rubbed Victor's hair.

"What do you mean dad?" asked Victor with a shocked expression on his face.

"Do you not think I know?" said Freddie as he gave a small laugh.

"Know what?" said Victor as he tried to avoid all possible eye contact with his dad.

"That you like men. I'm not stupid you know. I know you better than you know yourself I want you to know that. I've always known. I probably found out before you did."

"Did Edna tell you?" cried Victor.

"No, Edna did not tell me. Plus I overheard your conversation with her when you told her you were gay. And my suspicions were finally laid to rest. I knew. I never told your mum. I wanted her to find out by herself by either you telling her or her finding out the same way I did."

Victor was speechless.

"Come on. We can't stay here forever. We need to get to the forest. I have a new plan. But first I'm going to get the shotgun from upstairs. I want you to stay here and not move from here. It is far too dangerous for you to go upstairs."

"Okay," Freddie stood up and started to walk to the stairs, "Dad?" Freddie turned around as he picked up the revolver and he nodded, "I'm sorry. I do love you. I...it's just..."

Freddie wrapped his arms around him and brought him close to his chest and said, "It's okay. You had every right to be angry with me and what I had done. You don't need to explain yourself to me. Listen, we just gotta stick to together. If we do that. We'll live."

Victor could only nod as a response his eyes were

tearing up, "Let's swap," said Freddie as he offered him his revolver. Victor looked up, his eyes went wide. "Take it," Victor took the gun and handed Freddie the knife, "I'm going to get the shotgun. When I have it. I'm going to come back and we will discuss the plan." "Okay, dad."
Freddie held the knife and he started to walk up the stairs. He looked back when he reached the top and nodded to Victor.
"When we get out of here Vic, I'm taking you for your first beer in Orington. God knows we need one after what we've been through," he laughed and said, "Seriously, I promise. We will get out of here. Together."

5

Freddie Martin slowly closed the door to the cellar behind him.
The snow had started to build up inside the house from when Agatha tore her way inside. He looked outside, there was nothing but darkness and the howling of the wind.
Freddie shivered, he kept a tight grip of the kitchen knife in his hand. And made sure the blade was pointed outwards.
The entire house was a mess. It had been torn into and destroyed. Agatha had thrown some chairs into the hallway from the dining room. When she followed them in there last night, he peered through the door. Inside the place was a mess. The table had been thrown into the kitchen door with such force the table has split almost in two.
How could such a thing happen to them?
Freddie entered the cupboard that was in the kitchen

wall, he pulled items out of the way and kept his eyes darting around the room every time he moved something. He didn't want Agatha or Heather to come in. He was quiet and moved with ease.

Once he found the wooden box leaning on the wall he pulled it free. It was heavy, just as he had expected. He quickly placed it on the countertop in the kitchen and unclipped the hinges on either side. Once he opened it a double-barrelled shotgun was lying on it's back. Staring up at him. He grinned as he pulled it up from the velvet cushion it had been lying on for the past twenty years. He had never used it. It had belonged to his father. It had his initials carved into the stock: J.M.

He smiled and removed the gun and snapped it open, he turned back to the cupboard and looked for the shells, he moved box after box, coat after coat. Then he found it. A cardboard box, he flipped the lid open with his thumb and there was five up and five down. He removed two of the shells and placed them in the shotgun before snapping it closed. He quickly pulled back the hammers and headed back to the cellar. The shotgun in one hand and the shells in the other. His mind was taken back to Victor. His third child and second son with Gwenda. That boy was truly something, no wonder why he was the favourites. Yes, Freddie knew that he shouldn't be picking favourites out of his children. But he was the only child that didn't do anything that Freddie was ashamed of. The boy was both brave and intelligent. He loved his other children, at the end of the day he was human. He was allowed to choose who was his favourite over the others. As a father or even a mother, every parent had their favourite child, no arguments about that.

He sometimes wondered why parents always said that they didn't have a favourite child. They did.

As a father, he could say that. But it didn't mean he didn't love his other children any less, even Heather. He raised her as his own, he loved that little girl and to find out she wasn't his did more than break his heart. Victor must have seen the pain in his eyes when Gwenda confessed to her sin. Saying how God had turned his back on them, for an event such as this to take over the farm.

That was when he saw something, it was footprints. Bloody and muddy footprints going upstairs. The feet were small and could have only belonged to Victor. He sighed and looked at the steps, each of them had a footprint. Freddie decided to go up.

He followed them and they lead to the spare bedroom at the end of the hallway. He placed the shells down and slowly raised the shotgun, he was expecting Thomas to jump out with the crossbow. He hadn't heard from them for a while now. He presumed they had died, from the constant screaming and then the dead silence. It was the only logical thing that could have happened to them. Freddie did feel a need to go upstairs and see if it was true, but he couldn't. The fear of seeing his eldest son lying dead was too strong. Something he didn't want to experience, he had seen too much tonight. No one else was going to die.

Freddie twisted the handle to the spare bedroom and pushed the door open with the shotgun, he raised the gun and aimed it inside. The room was dark and cold.

He licked his dry lips and stepped inside, once he looked around something moved from the other side of the bed. Freddie aimed the shotgun in that direction.

167

He gritted his teeth, ready to fire.

Then two hands wrapped around the bedpost and a small figure came out. He heard the blood tapping on the floor and when he turned his head. He saw it was Toby.

The boy looked at his dad and spoke, "Dad, look what you did!"

Freddie began to lower the shotgun, "I didn't mean too hurt you, Toby. I swear. It was an accident!"

"It's your fault!"

"No, it's not!"

"It's your fault! It's your fault! It's your fault! It's your fault! It's your fault!" Toby began to scream the three words over and over again.

"No!" cried Freddie as he raised the shotgun.

Toby made a hissing sound, similar to that of a snake. He began to stand but he didn't extend his legs or anything like that. Two spider like legs had grown out of his back and lifted his body in the darkness.

His mouth opened up and exposed sharp teeth, his mouth looked like it belonged to an anglerfish!

He reached out his arms, Freddie lifted the shotgun as high as he could and pulled the two triggers as hard as he could.

BANG! BANG!

There was a loud splattering sound after that followed by a heavy thud. Freddie looked down, Toby lay on his side. His head had exploded leaving just his tongue and a few teeth left in the remains of his gums.

Freddie let out a cry and pulled himself out of the bedroom before heading down the stairs. He needed to get to Victor and discuss what the two of them would do next. Freddie snatched up the shotgun shells and as quickly and as quietly as he could. He headed down the

stairs, noticing how the bloody footprints had gone. Like his guilt for killing Toby. He had ended his guilt.
It was over

6

Victor Martin remained alone in the cellar. He was sitting on top of one of the large wooden boxes. The revolver was in his hand. He would pass it to the other to pass the time now and again. His mum lay still and he would look at her now and again.
Then he heard a noise coming from the window. It sounding like a bag of marbles being shaken. It disturbed him.
He slowly pulled the hammer of the revolver back and looked up towards the window. He felt the weight of the revolver, the beating of his heart and the fear in his veins.

7

Freddie reached the door to the cellar, he grabbed the handle and slowly twisted it. Once he flung it open he saw Victor standing at the bottom of the stairs, he had his back to him and he was pointing the revolver at the window.
Victor turned around and shouted, "Behind you!"
Freddie turned around, he saw the pale bloody face of Agatha come towards him. He didn't know why he did it, but he did. He ducked. He threw his body to the side and he landed near the chest of drawers. He watched as Agatha's body flew through the cellar door towards Victor, Freddie shouted, "Oh no! Oh god! Oh shit!"
Freddie threw himself upwards and ran to the door, Victor was pulling himself backwards he aimed the

revolver and fired at Agatha but missed.
"Dad! Help me! Please!" cried Victor.
He was getting closer to the boxes now.
Then something came through the window. Freddie
knew what it was. It was Heather. She was crawling on
the wall and running towards Victor, "Dad! For the love
of God! Help me! Please!"
Freddie stood still with fear, the shotgun was lying on
the floor and the shells spilled across the ground.
Then he grabbed the door to the cellar and slammed it
shut.
"Dad!"
Victor lifted the revolver and fired at Heather, the bullet
missed and struck the wall. Tears were streaming down
his eyes now as he only had two bullets left.
He pulled back the hammer, blisters forming on his
trigger finger and his thumb. He pulled the trigger. The
revolver barked and Victor dropped it on the floor, in a
panic he stumbled and fell in between two creates, he
was like a cork in a wine bottle.
He reached for the revolver and pulled it up, but as
Agatha lunged towards he pulled the trigger. It was as a
reaction and a fear of dying that did that. He saw as the
bullet tore through his knee cap. Blood exploded into the
air. Agatha towered over him and Heather was on the
wall above his head.
"Dad! Please! I'm going to die!"
The two of them jumped on top of him.
All Freddie could hear was Victor's blood-curdling
screams.

8

That was it.

Freddie was the last one left alive of the Martin farm.
He pressed his body against the wall near the door and
listened as Victor's screams eventually died out.
What had he done?
Freddie had fucked up.
He then started to cry, his eyes welling up with tears as
they streamed down his cheeks. Creating clear paths in
the blood and in the dirt that had stained his skin
throughout the day. He punched the floor when he knew
that Victor was dead. What had he done?
He broke a promise that was what he had done.
Freddie had to go through with his plan no matter what
happened. He had no choice, he couldn't die. He had to
tell the story of what had happened here.
Freddie limped into the kitchen and stopped near the gas
cooker, he turned on the gas on all four of the hobs.
He pulled a chair under the bulb in the kitchen and with
his hand he began to squeeze the bulb. His hand turned
into a fist as the glass began to crack. He popped it and
as he pulled his hand away he brushed the glass from his
palm and from in between his fingers. He replaced his
thin coat with a warm jacket and he zipped it up.
There was no time for gloves, he tucked the shotgun
under his arm and headed to the kitchen door.
Freddie flicked the switch.
A few seconds later the kitchen and dining room
exploded.

9

Freddie started to run as fast as he could through the
blizzard, the snow was hammering down on his body as
he wrapped his arms around himself. His boots were
sinking into the snow after every step he took. He

wanted to make sure he was as far away from the house as possible. He could smell the burning, hear the flames crackling and feel the heat on his back. He turned his head and the entire bottom floor seemed to be a light. Flames roared around the building as it started to consume the large farmhouse.

He heard the farm as she cried out, as her walls gave in, as her floorboards collapsed. As other parts of the house began to tear open from the small and large bursts of fire that roared through the halls and walls.

He watched, he stared as the blizzard made the house slowly disappear. He could only see the orange glow in the distance, but that soon started to fade.

He heard the house finally when the roof collapsed and crushed the lower floors of the house. Destroying anything in the way, He heard it.

It brought a tear to his eye, knowing he had to kill his own house to save himself.

Victor...

He slammed that door shut and just sat there listening to his son as he screamed for him to help him. Screaming as Agatha and Heather started to kill him and strip the flesh from his bones.

Freddie didn't want to be thinking about it. Thinking what had killed him, Victor never deserved to die in the way he did. He should be with him now as they walked across the field and towards the tree line. The walk to the forest was a blind one, he knew he was close when he would be able to see the shooting range. That had to be close sooner or later. He just hoped he hadn't gotten lost and something had started to follow him!

No, he was sure they were all dead. The Brent brothers had been killed by himself and Edna.

Heather and Agatha had been burnt alive and Toby had
been shot in the head. No one else had turned.
As for Thomas. Well, he wasn't sure what had happened
to him. He just hoped his death was peaceful.

10

He had done it.
Freddie reached the gun range, he placed the shotgun
down and leaned on the side of it. He was tired. The
only sounds he could now hear was the whistling of the
wind. And feel the coldness as it blew around his face
and made his entire body shiver. The strong winds had
blown his hood down, it was too powerful for him to
bring back up. Once he managed to catch his breath he
picked up the shotgun and headed down the hill. His feet
hammered into the floor to ensure he didn't slip, it had
almost been glazed with ice over the passing hours.
He reached the bottom and lifted his hand, and he saw
his wedding ring. It was golden and smooth looking.
He ran his hand over it and whispered, "Gwenda..."
He did love her and at one point she did love him, her
love for him had slowly started to die away over the
years. Things like that happened. He knew that. His own
parents had stopped loving one another but lived
together and acted like good friends. They stayed
together for the sake of Freddie, he was told that once by
his father after his mother has passed away during that
storm. It seemed like a lifetime ago since hat had
happened to him, he was the last surviving Martin.
He stopped near a tree and he was cold, numb and
growing more tired, he pressed his back on the bark and
slid down the floor. The shotgun was pointed in the air.
He kept his hand near the trigger, ready to fire in case

something was to happen to him.

For now, he was free, free and away from the horrors that had unfolded on his farm on a 24 hour period.

He lost his family in one day, each of them consumed by a monster that seemed to be from hell itself.

His love for them all remained intact, and although he would not like to admit it. He loved Gwenda Swan too. He could remember the first time they met at the Crossbow pub in Orington. She was so beautiful, himself and his friends were drinking pints of lager. Then he noticed her, sitting at the bar with one of her friends. She was drinking some shandy. When she turned around their eyes locked and she smiled at him before turning away and continuing with her drink,

"Ey up. Freddie boy has some woman over there looking at him," said Roger as he nudged Edward on his arm.

"What? Really?" said Edward.

"Yeah really. Look at his face. He's obsessed with her. You are in there mate. Go on. Go talk to her."

"I know. I know. Just give me time. I'm going to play her for a bit first," said Freddie as he took a mouthful of his pint.

"Play her? What do you think this is Monopoly? Go and talk to her. Or I will?" said Roger as he pulled his stool backwards using his feet.

"You? Oh, come on Roger. You've got more chance of finding Lord Lucan over a woman," said Edward as he slapped his leg.

Edward was always one for cracking jokes no matter what the situation was. He did miss them two. They no longer lived in Orington. They both moved away with their wives. Edward went first, he moved down to

Oxford. Roger was next, he moved down to Devon with his wife. Last time he heard about them both, they had children. Freddie was invited to both weddings but he couldn't attend. The farm was too important and he couldn't trust his farmhands to maintain it whilst he was gone. The Brent brothers were assigned back then. It was two other men who moved back to Orington when they found better work.

"I have had girlfriends you know!" exclaimed Roger.

"Yeah, and she went back to school last week. Shut up. So, are you going to talk to her then Freddie boy?"

"Yeah, just give me a moment Ed."

"I will my friend. Who wants another pint then?" said Edward.

"Yeah go on," said Roger as he handed a five-pound note to Edward.

"Freddie?"

"Nah, I'll get myself one when her friend goes away." Edward nodded and headed to the bar. He ordered two pints of lager lime and then brought the two golden fizzy pints back with a frothy top.

Freddie waited for around 20 minutes until Gwenda's friend got up to have a smoke outside. Freddie sat next to her and introduced himself, they spoke to one another for a while. He offered to walk her home and the two of them walked home. Hand in hand.

"What do you do for a living Freddie?" asked Gwenda as the night air blew around the two of them.

"I work on my father's farm. It's on the outskirts of Orington."

"Oh, you are the heir to a farm? That's interesting."

"I am, I work full time. Weekends off. And what do you do Gwenda?"

"I work as a barmaid. At the Crossbow. It's not much, but like you, I get weekends off."

"It's better than nothing. I always wanted to be an explorer when growing up. I then realised I had to help my father. Family is important to me. So are friends."

"I couldn't agree more."

The two of them chatted all the way home, they reached her cottage and two of them sat on the kerb.

They chatted until the early hours of the morning,

"It's five in the morning," said Freddie with laughter.

"And you have to walk back to the farm? How long will that take?"

"Around an hour. I have done it countless times before dear."

"Why don't you sleep mine?" she said nervously.

"Are you sure?"

"No. But I'm willing to see how you are," she said as she grabbed his hand.

She was so beautiful, he couldn't get that out his head. The two of them entered her bedroom and the two lay on her bed. They never made love but they braced one another. They only made love a year into their relationship. He wasn't a virgin. And neither was she, but they were both inexperienced. So the act was that of awkwardness but it was love-filled too.

He held her in the bed and kissed her cheek.

By morning the two of them shared a pot of tea and fresh pancakes.

That was how it all started between them and he would have had it no other way. She was his everything and he would do anything for her. They had Thomas 18 years ago in April. He was a beautiful baby boy. He was a good child. And so was the remaining children. The more he thought of it, Heather was the worst experience he had had with the children. She was crying all the time and refused to eat and sleep, she would empty her bowls in her nappies most of the time.

Once she reached her toddler years she seemed to calm down a little. As Freddie began to look after her more and more. She bonded with Freddie more than Gwenda. But Gwenda didn't seem to care. And that hurt him.

He watched as Heather would come to him when she hurt herself or when she wanted something.

Freddie was always there by her side and you know what, he truly loved that little girl as his own. He thought she was his, but it didn't change a thing. Hugo was never the father in the situation and never admitted to it. He wasn't a man, more of a mouse.

Freddie and Gwenda's marriage was healthy for some years. They had their odd argument here and there but it was nothing to cause any cracks. Freddie didn't realise at the time that the arguments were rather causing chips, not cracks.

He felt a strain around three months before Toby's death. The crushing weight then landed on the two of them when that combine ripped him open. That was how their life was. He enjoyed the whisky and she enjoyed the company of other men because he couldn't provide for her.

It was funny, for the past 20 years he had never thought about Roger and Edward. He wondered how the two of them were doing now. Had their marriages lasted like his own? Had they moved on and married other women? Were they alive? Were they dead?

Freddie had so many questions and no answers to give to any of them. Friends were just as important as family

and without any of them. Who are you?
He lowered his head as the snow began to pick up. He
rubbed his eyes and checked the shotgun, he snapped it
open, placed in two shells and had other ideas.
He slipped the two barrels into his mouth, feeling the
cold metal touching the back of his throat. The gun was
rather large and very difficult to fit into his mouth. But
he managed to slip it in between his fat lips.
His numb fingers reached down for the hammer, he
grabbed them and pulled them both back. He was sure
the blast at this range would blow his head apart.
He was-
NO!
He pulled the shotgun out from his mouth and threw it
as far away as he could. He heard it strike a tree, before
smashing into the snow and being quickly buried as the
blizzard started the pick up now. The wind howled like a
wolf and the snow sliced through flesh like musket
balls.
Freddie feared crying, he was scared in case his eyes
froze over. But instead, he placed his hands upon his
face and sobbed. It was all he could do. He cried.
He was ready to wipe his eyes with his fingers but he
couldn't move his hands. He couldn't move them!
Oh god!
He pulled and he pulled.
But they didn't budge. His hands had fused to his face.
His screams were muffled by his hands. His fingers
blocked his eyesight.
Freddie Martin didn't realise it.
But he was now within the eyes of darkness.

February 2020

Authors notes

The idea of In the eyes of darkness had been beating around my head for a few months. I had no idea how to approach the idea. At first, the family consisted of four members. But the idea grew bigger and bigger. The story got deeper and deeper. Until I finished it in April of 2019. But the story wasn't what I wanted it to be.
So I started again. This is the finished product.
Although this is just a novella I think every book that is written requires help from numerous people. No just the author themselves. I would like to thank Keanu Jones, Nathan Neville, Jake Powell-Foster and Gemma Roberts. Thanks for letting me come to you with updates about this story.